Spies Like Us

Spies

LIKE US

By
KATHY IVAN

COPYRIGHT

Spies Like Us – Copyright © January 2017 by Kathy Ivan

Cover by Kim Killion and The Killion Group, Inc.

Release date: January 2017
Print Edition

All Rights Reserved

NEWSLETTER SIGN UP

Thank you so much for reading my book. If you want to find out about my other books, new releases, contests, free reads, and other things that are going on, sign up for my newsletter at http://eepurl.com/baqdRX

I take your privacy seriously. I will not sell your e-mail or contact you for any other reason than to send you publication updates when a new release is available.

BOOKS BY KATHY IVAN

www.kathyivan.com/books.html

NEW ORLEANS CONNECTION SERIES

Desperate Choices

Connor's Gamble

Relentless Pursuit

Ultimate Betrayal

Keeping Secrets

Sex, Lies and Apple Pies

Deadly Justice

Saving Sarah

(part of Susan Stoker's Special Forces Kindle World)

Deadly Obsession

Hidden Agenda

Saving Savannah

(part of Susan Stoker's Special Forces Kindle World)

Spies Like Us

Fatal Intentions (coming February 2017)

LOVIN' LAS VEGAS SERIES

It Happened In Vegas

Crazy Vegas Love

Marriage, Vegas Style

A Virgin In Vegas

Vegas, Baby!

Yours For The Holidays

Match Made In Vegas

Wicked Wagers (box set books 1-4)

OTHER BOOKS BY KATHY IVAN

Second Chances (Destiny's Desire Book #1)
Losing Cassie (Destiny's Desire Book #2)
The Remingtons: Could This Be Love
(Part of Melissa Foster's Kindle World)

Dear Reader,

Welcome to The Big Easy!

Spies Like Us is the latest book in my New Orleans Connection series. This story was written for all the fans who've asked for more of Gator Boudreau and Ms. Willie. I've received so many e-mails wanting to see more of these two characters, because there's something about the older couple's special background that screamed for them to be together. This book is for you. I hope I didn't disappoint.

In the New Orleans series, you'll find a unique blend of suspense, romance, and intrigue set in the heart of New Orleans, filled with alpha heroes oozing Southern charm and the strong women they love. So, sit back and hold on tight for a roller coaster ride of nail-biting intrigue, sensual tension, and a touch of humor with Spies Like Us.

And if you love contemporary romance with a comedic flair, check out my Loviin' Las Vegas series.

Laissez les bons temps rouler!

Kathy Ivan

Chapter One

How had he gotten dragged into this mess? Oh, yeah. He answered his phone.

"Gator, I realized you were the perfect person to call with my little problem." Abigail Benedict passed him a cup of tea. *Hot tea.* In a dainty, girly cup he was afraid would shatter into a million pieces in his ham-handed grip. Gritting his teeth, he gave her a weak smile, eyeing the cardboard-looking, store-bought cookies on a plate in the middle of the table.

"Start at the beginning, Abigail. Tell me everything."

"It happened a couple of weeks ago. This nice man stopped by, collecting toys for the children at the homeless shelters and women's shelters. For Christmas." She paused, taking a sip of her tea.

"You didn't find it unusual for somebody to come knocking on your door, asking for toys?"

"Not at all. He seemed very nice. Besides, Henrietta from church gave him my name and address." Abigail smiled benignly, though it didn't quite reach her eyes. Eyes which always reminded him of a basset hound, with their droopy lids and sad expression. "She knows how much I love kids, though Joshua and I were never blessed with any of our own."

Not much he could say to that, was there? Instead, he shoved a cookie into his mouth, nearly choking on its dry, brittle texture. He hated to admit it, but he'd gotten spoiled on the goodies at Carpenter's office. He'd even started showing up there when there wasn't a legitimate reason, just to see what Carpenter's beguiling housekeeper whipped up for the employees.

Wilhelmina McDaniels, known to everybody as Ms. Willie, treated each one of Carpenter's elite team members like they were her own children. Now, every time he popped in, she shoved food at him, too. *Damned fine cookies too, and cinnamon buns, and those lemon scones…umm.*

"Gator, are you listening?"

"Sorry, Abigail, just thinking about what you said. This man only asked for toys? Not cash?"

"Oh, no, Gator. The donations were for new, un-wrapped toys only." As he watched, a flush crept into her cheeks, though it was hard to distinguish in the almost eighty-year-old woman, her face creased with the lines and wrinkles of a life well-lived.

"And?"

"Well, I told him I didn't have any toys, seeing as I never had children. That's when he told me I could donate money to buy some."

Ah, hell. He was beginning to think Abigail had been conned by a pro. Prey to a shill trolling for his next elderly mark. Usually sharp as a tack, his elderly neighbor had a soft spot for kids. Every year, come Halloween, the whole area swarmed with costumed hooligans making a beeline for her front porch, because she gave them enough candy to induce a sugar coma.

"Did you give him money?"

"No. It was the end of the month, and I didn't have any cash on hand. But he did say I could make a donation at the Santa's Village."

"Santa's Village?" He nearly gave in to the urge to roll his eyes, and prayed for strength. Was this about to turn into a bigger fiasco than he'd assumed? "Which one?"

Little holiday shops sprang up all over the parishes from November first through the end of the year. Some of them were nothing more than a series of small booths with a Santa Claus and a photographer. Others were elaborate displays, complete with elves and live reindeer.

"The Santa's Village at The Grand Escape. It takes over the entire first floor. It's really lovely, Gator. Have you seen it? All decorated for the holidays, it's set up for families and children to visit."

The Grand Escape was one of the larger hotels not too far from the French Quarter. It catered to convention goers, large conferences, and family vacationers. They had assorted activities for children and adults, making it a very popular place for locals and tourists alike. While it was part of a large chain of hotels, each one utilized the unique atmosphere and ambience of its locale to make it a one-of-a-kind experience. The Grand Escape New Orleans featured things like a Mardi Gras room, a riverboat attraction, and extensive gardens reminiscent of New Orleans' famous Garden District.

"Abigail, please tell me you didn't give them money."

"Of course, I did, dear. I couldn't let those poor children go without presents at Christmas. What kind of a Christian woman would I be if I saw a need and didn't do my best to help?"

"How much did you give them?" *Please say a small amount.* Though if his gut was a barometer, the mercury had just bottomed out and storm clouds were billowing on the horizon.

"Well, that's where the problem comes in, dear. I gave them twenty-five dollars." She took another sip of tea before setting the cup on the table. "I wrote them a check."

Holy crap on a cracker. A check?

"What happened next?"

"I went to the grocery store and tried to pay with my debit card, but the transaction wouldn't go through. I contacted the bank, and they said…they said all my money was gone!"

Tears began rolling down her wrinkled cheeks, and the sobs she tried to muffle nearly broke his heart. He handed her the napkin she'd placed beside his tea cup earlier, and she blotted her cheeks.

"When I called Henrietta, she said the same thing happened to her too. Another woman in the church said their account was depleted—empty."

Gator drew in a deep sigh, knowing what he had to do, because he'd be damned if he'd allow some two-bit swindler to come in and take advantage of the elderly in his parish.

"Okay, Abigail, let me look into this and see if I can

figure out what's going on. First, did the man give you his name?"

Abigail's brow scrunched in concentration. "I don't remember. I'm sure he did, but…my memory isn't what it used to be."

"What did he look like? Can you describe him for me?"

Her expression brightened immediately. "Oh, yes. I do remember what he looked like. Very distinctive."

Gator waited, hoping she'd get to the point. When she didn't say anything, he prompted, "He looked like…"

"An elf, dear." Smiling, she patted his hand. "He looked like one of Santa's elves."

Chapter Two

Willie dropped her e-reader onto her lap at the hard banging on her front door. Damn and blast, she'd just gotten to the juicy bit too. Whoever it was, it better be bloody important to pull her away from Sarah Sloane's latest erotic thriller.

Tossing aside the afghan she'd draped across her legs, she strode toward the door, determined to get rid of whoever interrupted her *me time*. This was her quiet hour, the part of the day she cherished. Her boys headed to their apartments or homes outside the building, and she relaxed with a nice cuppa and a good book.

Not bothering to look through the peephole, she flung the door open. After all, she lived above Carpenter Security Services. Nobody got into this building who wasn't supposed to be there. Nobody.

Oops, maybe I should have looked first.

Gator Boudreau stood in the hall, towering over her by several inches. A frown marred his face, one she secretly found attractive, though she'd never let on—not to anybody. Especially not to Miss Andrea, who'd recently decided to play matchmaker and kept trying to fix her up with dates. While she herself might play matchmaker for the younger

6

crew at Carpenter Security, any chance for romance had long since passed her by.

"Mr. Boudreau? Can I help you?" She held onto the solid wooden door, thankful for its extra support. Truth be told, she felt a little weak in the knees, with him standing on her doorstep, his gaze raking her from head to toe in a single sweep. A tingle raced along her spine, urging her to invite him inside.

"I've got a problem, and I'm hoping you can help."

"Of course. Please, come in." She made a nervous gesture, and he walked inside her private sanctuary. Rarely did anybody cross her threshold—except for the men of Carpenter Security Services and Mister Samuel, the owner of the company and the man she'd raised for most of his life.

Quickly heading for the sofa, she picked up the hand-crocheted afghan she'd received from her sister-in-law as a Christmas present, and folded it over her arm. Snatching up the e-reader, her fingertip slid across the button and closed her book, watching to see if he noticed. Wouldn't that be embarrassing, to have Gator Boudreau catch a glimpse of what she was reading? Even though it had been penned by his brand new daughter-in-law, it was an erotic thriller. She doubted he'd ever read a single one of Sarah's books. A surge of heat bled into her cheeks.

"Can I get you anything?" Taking a deep breath, she fell back on deeply ingrained proper British manners, drilled from her youth on how to be the perfect hostess.

"I wouldn't say no to a cup of coffee."

"I think I can manage that." With a smile, she turned

toward the kitchen. She couldn't help noticing Gator followed behind, easing his tall frame onto one of the leather-padded barstools lining the white quartz peninsula. Mister Samuel had given her free reign when the apartment was being renovated, and she'd done her best to make the space comfortable, adding her own personal stamp over every inch.

Reaching into an upper cupboard, she pulled out two mugs, knowing instinctively he wouldn't want one of the smaller, more fragile cups she normally used. Oh, no, Gator Boudreau epitomized masculinity. He wasn't overtly muscular, but she imagined beneath the denim jacket and black T-shirt, sinewy muscles roped his biceps and forearms. *Whew, is it getting hot in here?*

"What can I do for you, Mr. Boudreau?"

Running a hand along his jaw, he scratched lightly at the slight five o'clock shadow decorating his cheeks, the salt and pepper scruff giving him a gruff appearance. "First, call me Gator."

Another wave of heat flashed into her cheeks. "Okay, Gator. You said you needed my help?" She kept busy, getting the sugar bowl and creamer out and placing them on the countertop. During their staff meetings, she'd noted he added both to his coffee, though she wasn't about to admit she'd picked up on that little trait.

Passing him the first mug, she placed hers into the now-empty slot, and popped in a pod of her favorite french vanilla blend. Instinct made her place the cookie jar within his reach, lifting off the lid. Couldn't resist a tiny smile as his hand dug deep, pulled two of the chocolate chip cookies out, and took a big bite. A touch of pride suffused her at his look of pleasure.

"I've got a problem. Well, not me personally, but a friend, who's been swindled out of her life savings. She and several other elderly women."

She took a sip of coffee, watching him over the rim of her cup. The look of determination on his face sent a tingle racing up her spine. What would it be like to have that kind of focus directed at her? She nearly choked on her coffee at the wild thought. Good grief, when had her libido ratcheted into high gear? Though she knew the answer to that question—the day she'd laid eyes on Gator Boudreau. *Get back on track, or he's going to think you've lost your mind.*

"Swindled? What happened?"

"Don't have all the details yet, but an elderly neighbor called me, asking for help. Seems somebody came to her door looking for donations for the kids at the local women's and homeless shelters. Claimed they were collecting for Christmas gifts."

"A worthwhile charitable contribution, though I'm assuming it wasn't legitimate?"

She watched him take another bite of cookie, after dunking it into his coffee, and hid her smile behind her cup. It was a sensual feast, watching this man. His smile did something to her insides, even if it was only due to the taste of chocolate and brown sugar. Shoot, she'd probably melt into a puddle if he ever turned all that primal attention on her.

"The man said they were collecting new unwrapped toys. Since she didn't have any, Abigail asked about donating money. The guy said donations could be made at the Santa's Village at The Great Escape."

"The posh hotel? I haven't been there since moving here, but I visited the one in Dallas."

He nodded. "Yeah, the chain does big business nationally. Anyway, they decorate the whole place for the holidays, and allow local vendors to set up shops. Entertaining for the kids, and it brings extra money and attention to local craftsmen who really need the recognition."

She cocked her head. "Doesn't Mister Samuel own a good portion of The Great Escape chain? I believe I've heard him mention them once or twice."

"Don't know. I don't keep track of where he gets his money." Gator chuckled, and the sound sent another shiver racing down her spine. "I still remember him as the wet-behind-the-ears kid who came home from school with Jean-Luc. It's hard picturing any of my boys being grown adults."

She had met his four strapping lads, all ex-military, and every one of them now working for Carpenter Security Services. She'd yet to meet his daughter, who was attending college. Unless the lass showed up at the office, she'd probably never get the opportunity.

"I take it your neighbor went to the Santa's Village and made a monetary donation?"

"Wrote them a check."

She winced at the harshness in his tone, though she fully agreed. Didn't people think before they did stupid things? Probably not, or they wouldn't do them. "I didn't think anybody wrote checks anymore. There's so much information available on those little pieces of paper. Account numbers, routing numbers, names and addresses, and sometimes even telephone numbers. Anybody who's halfway proficient with a computer—"

"Can rob you blind? That's exactly what happened to Abigail and the other ladies from her church. Each one found their checking accounts emptied."

"Oh, dear." Gently placing her cup on the counter, she started to reach into the cookie jar, stopping herself just in time. The last thing she needed was a fattening, calorie-laden, mouthful of chocolatey goodness. Nope, she'd struggled too hard to lose those forty pounds. And she wasn't done yet. Those last stubborn ten pounds weren't coming off easily, but she was determined.

"I've got a plan to see if this is just a coincidence, which I doubt, or if some con artist is using the holidays to take advantage of the elderly women in my parish."

She immediately noted his emphasis of the word *my* when talking about both the women and the parish. The man loved New Orleans and the surrounding bayous and her citizens. And its people loved him in return. Opened up to him when they wouldn't talk to anybody else. Didn't matter if it was the mayor of the city or a homeless vet living on the riverfront—everybody knew they could confide in Gator Boudreau.

"What can I do to help?"

He got a look on his face, one she recognized from all the time she'd spent watching Mister Samuel growing up. It was that I'm-gonna-ask-you-something-but-I-don't-think-you'll-like-it face.

"I've lined up a job, part-time, working at the Santa's Village at The Great Escape. But there's a catch that's a little...unusual. That's where you come in."

Well, well, look at that. She hadn't known the man could blush, yet a hint of pink stained his cheeks.

"Sounds like a good idea. Being Johnny-on-the-spot will make investigating these corrupt people easier." She leaned her hip against the corner of the peninsula, and studied him closely. Saw the minute shifting in his seat before he pulled his shoulders back and placed his mug on the counter.

"I agree. Here's my dilemma. The job I've got actually requires two people, and I'm hoping you'll fill the other slot." His words came out in a rush, running together where she almost didn't understand him.

"A two-man operation? Isn't that a bit unusual for a holiday position?" Not that she'd know. She'd worked for the Carpenter family ever since Mister Samuel's grandfather hired her to be the little man's nanny and bodyguard. That job alone had taken up all her time.

"Here's the thing. I did a bit of fast talking with the woman who runs the Santa's Village in order to get this gig. A few bribes might have changed hands. I need to be on-site in order to investigate, see if others have been taken advantage of, or if this was an isolated thing, targeting only older members of the church."

Maybe she was being dense, but she still didn't under-stand what he wanted.

"Gator, what exactly do you need from me?"

Steely blue eyes met hers. "I need you to be my wife."

Chapter Three

Shoving the over-stuffed pillowy lining into the front of his pants, Gator buttoned then belted the fur-trimmed red jacket with the wide black leather belt, cinching it closed. His gaze went straight to the fake white beard lying on the table in front of him.

I look like an idiot. A six foot one, hundred and eighty-five pound laughingstock. What in the hell had he gotten himself into?

Looping the elastic over his ears to hold the fake beard in place, he settled the red felt hat with its attached white wig atop his head, scowling. Blast Abigail and her blasted friends. Only good thing about the outfit—it was warm. The Santa's Village section they'd cordoned off for the kids to sit on Santa's—his—lap was located right next to the entrance for the giant ice sculptures. For the first hour, he'd nearly frozen his butt off before he could take a break and put a long-sleeved shirt on beneath the jolly fat man's red jacket. Next time, he was wearing flannel underwear.

"You know, when you asked me to be your wife, I really wasn't expecting this." His eyes flew to the mirror in front of him and spotted Wilhelmina McDaniels, decked out in her Mrs. Claus outfit. Damn, if she didn't fill it out in all the right places. He had to swallow before he could respond.

"Makes perfect sense. Mr. and Mrs. Claus don't stand out in a Santa's Village as unusual. Gives us the perfect excuse for being here, and gets us into places a civilian can't go."

"Including the donation site for the fraudulent charity." She tugged on the ties at the front of her corset she wore over her dress, and he chuckled softly. Guess she didn't like her costume any more than he did, though she might change her mind if she realized how stunning she looked wearing the outfit. The red velvet dress hugged her curves in all the right places, and the white frilly apron over the top nipped in her waist. The woman was built just the way he liked, voluptuous, with curves that went on for miles. He'd watched her drop a lot of pounds since moving to New Orleans, and he secretly hoped she wouldn't lose any more, because she looked perfect.

A twinge of guilt assailed him. Though he'd dated off and on since his wife, Elizabeth, had passed, Wilhelmina was the first woman he'd been attracted to on more than just a physical basis. The woman had a mind like a steel trap, and a sharp wit that kept everyone on their toes. It didn't hurt that the sight of her revved his engine.

"I bribed the guy the hotel hired to originally play Santa. He was more than happy to take the money and run." He pointed to his outfit with a grimace. "Not that I blame him. I don't mind the kids. Hell, I love kids, but some of these parents are getting on my last nerve. And this fur itches."

She tugged at the mobcap sitting atop her head, blonde

curls peeking out from beneath its ruffled rim. "Were you able to get any further description of our con man from the other ladies?"

"Nothing useful. All three women I talked with remember their conversations with the guy, but when it comes to describing him, all they can remember is he wore a Santa's elf costume." He pointed toward the open doorway she'd come through. "There must be a dozen elves wandering around out there. I think every store in the place has at least one working for them."

"It does make our job a bit difficult, I'll admit." Her hands again toyed with the laces of the apron, untying and then retying the bow. "I'm having tea with one of the gals working at Holly Jolly Holiday Helpers during my lunch break. Hopefully, I can do a little discreet snooping."

Hmm, looks like my partner already made a few inroads of her own. He had to hand it to the British woman, she knew how to make people feel relaxed and comfortable around her.

"I'll tag along."

"No, no, that won't do at all." Reaching forward, she adjusted the white fuzzy ball at the end of his cap, before brushing her hands along his shoulders in a brisk, no-nonsense fashion. "This is a girls' gab fest. If you show up, they won't feel free to share a little gossip."

Fighting the urge to roll his eyes, instead he plunked the wire-rimmed glasses on the bridge of his nose, and looked at her over the top of the frames. "Fine. I'll wander around a bit, mosey into a couple of the shops. Nothing in the rule book says Santa can't do a bit of Christmas shopping."

"Well, actually…" She grinned and he felt a hard thunk right in the pit of his stomach. Not an unpleasant feeling, but one he wasn't used to, though he could easily put a name to it. *Desire.*

"Anybody asks, I can always say I'm looking for a little something for the missus."

"Well, if anybody asks, my favorite color is blue, and I prefer dark chocolate."

He grinned. "Got it." With a final tug on his coat, he offered his arm. "Come on, Mrs. Claus, we've got lists to check. Hopefully, most of these rug-rats aren't on the naughty one."

"We should be so lucky." Though she said it under her breath, he heard her words quite clearly. Well, well. Looked like he'd have to sweeten up Mrs. Claus' disposition. And maybe get a chance to find out a bit more about Miss Wilhelmina McDaniels in the process. The woman was an enigma, a complex puzzle—and there wasn't a puzzle invented Gator Boudreau couldn't crack.

This might be fun.

Chapter Four

Three hours. She'd been on her feet for the last three hours, herding children through the line, and up to sit on Santa's lap. Smiled pleasantly for the camera until her cheeks hurt. They actually ached.

Placing both hands on the small of her back, she stretched, working out the kinks. They'd just put up the sign, stating the Santa Booth was closed for the next hour, so they could have their meal break.

"You ready to get that tea, Willie?" Cheryl, the spunky redhead who worked at the candle shop strolled over, her dark forest green skirt swaying with each step. She'd met the younger woman the day before, during their orientation meeting, when she and Gator made the rounds of the facility and met the other shop owners.

"My dear, you have no idea how much I've been looking forward to a cuppa. Who knew standing for so long would wear a body out?"

"Me." Cheryl laughed. "I did the whole elf gig one year at the photo booth, and I don't think I sat down for three solid weeks."

"I'm still not sure how I let that man convince me to be Mrs. Claus."

Walking toward the coffee place located in the lobby area of The Great Escape, Cheryl pointed and they quickly slid into two empty seats.

"Let me go place our orders. I'll be right back." Willie watched the other woman's movements. She reminded her of a whirlwind, never still for more than a second, before she was shifting, swaying, or talking with her hands. Ah, the exuberance of youth. Not that she missed it all that much. She'd enjoyed her life and taking care of Samuel Carpenter had been a joy. One bright, shining moment in an otherwise abysmal time in her life. Looking back, her life started over the day she'd become nanny and bodyguard to Mister Samuel and his baby sister, Miss Lily.

"Wow, they're really busy here today. I love the holidays, though, don't you?" Cheryl flung herself in the chair across from Willie.

"Yes. There's something magical about the whole season, though I must confess I do miss not having a white Christmas."

"Do you get a lot of snow in London around the holidays?" Cheryl took a sip of her hot chocolate, and Willie wrapped her hands around her cup of tea, feeling the warmth slide over her fingers.

"Most years we get some. But I always spent Christmas and New Year's with my mum. She lived a couple of hours north of the city. A wee little cottage with a proper English garden." She spun the tale she always told whenever asked about her life in England. People wanted the fairy tale of the perfect childhood, with the thatched roof and wildflowers growing as far as the eye could see. Nobody wanted to hear about the single mother who'd tried to raise a child on the streets of an overcrowded city. Where there was never enough heat or food. Never enough money.

"I've lived here all my life, so I've never seen a white Christmas." Cheryl leaned forward. "Truthfully? I've only seen real snow once here, and it wasn't much." She shrugged, hair spilling across her shoulders in a cascade of fire. "Can't miss what you've never had, right?"

Willie took a sip of her tea, placed the cup down on the table, and added a spoonful of sugar. "I've been gone from London for a long time. I've been in the States for years, so I'm used to not seeing any measurable snowfall. The rest of the year, I'm more than happy to live in a warm climate."

"I guess. Can I ask you a question? You don't have to answer if you don't want to."

"Of course, dear. Ask me anything." She couldn't help wondering what had the younger girl all twitter-pated.

"I—you're here with Gator Boudreau."

Willie nodded, though she didn't speak, since it wasn't really a question. She had a feeling she'd already figured out what Cheryl wanted to ask.

"Do you think—I mean—never mind." Cheeks flushed, Cheryl quickly took another gulp of her hot chocolate, her gaze not meeting Willie's.

"Which one?"

Cheryl's gaze flew up and met hers, a question in her eyes.

"Which one of Gator's boys did you want to ask about?"

Willie smiled, wondering if the other woman's cheeks could flame any brighter. Oh, to be that young again.

"That obvious, huh?"

"When you've been around as long as I have, you learn to read the signs." Willie patted Cheryl's hand to soften her words. "Can't be Ranger, he's married. Let me think—Etienne, right?"

Cheryl's hands flew to her cheeks. "Am I that transparent?"

"Nonsense, dear. Etienne is a lovely young man. I've talked with him several times since he's been home."

Cheryl looked left and right before leaning closer. "He's so...I don't know how to describe it, but there's something about him..."

"That gets you all tongue-tied? Makes you feel tingly all over?"

Eyes downcast, Cheryl nodded mutely. *Poor girl.* Maybe she could have Etienne drop by and meet the young woman.

"Okay, time to change the subject before I spontaneously combust of embarrassment. So, you and Gator..."

It was Willie's turn to blush, flustered at the implication. "What? Oh, no, we're friends."

"Looked kinda cozy to me. Besides, he can't keep his eyes off you."

"Believe me, Cheryl, there's nothing between me and Gator Boudreau." She made the statement firm and decisive.

Cheryl rested her chin on her palm, elbow braced on the table. "Hmm, I think you're protesting a bit too much. Besides, he's a really nice guy. Everybody in New Orleans thinks he's great."

Something Willie had heard ad nauseam. To the people around Carpenter Security Services, the man walked on water. Though she had to admit, he'd been very useful in uncovering information that helped solve several of C.S.S.'s cases.

Gator Boudreau was a complicated man. And she'd know. One of the first things she'd done on moving to New Orleans with Mister Samuel was run a check on him. Called in several favors with her MI-5 contacts, because there was an underlying mystery beneath Gator Boudreau's façade. They'd turned up precisely—nothing. Nothing unusual. Fought in Vietnam at the tail end of that conflict. Worked a fishing boat for several years, had a wife and children. But she had her suspicions. She'd been too busy recently to follow through.

"Hey, ladies, mind if we join you?" A tall, thin woman of about forty stood beside Cheryl's chair, along with a perky blonde in a holly green elf costume. Perky seemed a fitting word, since she couldn't be more than eighteen or nineteen, and everything was still defying gravity.

"Sure, the more the merrier. Willie, meet Francine and Patti. Francine works the candy kiosk next to my shop, and has for the last four years. Patti works at Holly Jolly Holiday Helpers."

"Nice to meet you."

Willie watched Patti, feeling a tingle of excitement. Could little Ms. Perky be her ticket into Holly Jolly Holiday Helpers? She looked like she didn't have a brain in her head, but sometimes looks could be deceiving—she'd need to keep a close watch on Patti.

"This your first time at The Great Escape, Willie?" Francine asked, and she nodded, taking a sip of her tea. Meeting up with a couple of the other women might prove beneficial in weeding out the con man they suspected of bilking Abigail and her friends out of their money.

Francine leaned closer, her voice lowered to almost a whisper. "Please tell me that Santa's really Gator Boudreau. I swear, I only caught a glimpse, but it definitely looked like him."

Willie smiled. "Yes, it's him."

"Wow. Something big must be going on, because Gator doesn't do Christmas—ever." Francine punctuated her words with a huge grin. "Maybe he's finally ready to move on. Not that he's ever lacked female companionship when he wanted it, but nobody's ever gotten more than a date or two."

Willie's spine stiffened with each word the other woman spoke. She'd told Gator she wanted to find out the gossip, and try to get a lead on the confidence scam. Hearing gossip about him—that was a whole different thing. Even if this was fascinating gossip.

"Who's Gator?" Patti chimed in, a baffled expression on her face.

Francine rolled her eyes, and blew out an exasperated breath. "Gator Boudreau is the main man in New Orleans. You got a problem? You talk to Gator. You need help? You talk to Gator. He's Mister Fix-It."

"Well, my car's making this funny noise. Should I talk to Gator about that?"

Francine leaned forward, banging her forehead against the table top before straightening. "No, Patti. Gator doesn't do that kind of fixing. He fixes problems, like bullying. Or fighting city hall. Not engine repair—though he can probably do that too."

Willie started to speak, but her eye caught a flash of red across the area where they sat congregated around the tiny round table. Gator stood about six feet away, and when she caught his eye, he motioned for her.

"Looks like my break time's up. Ladies, it was a pleasure meeting you. Hopefully, we can do it again soon."

"Oh, you talk so pretty," Patti bounced in her seat, and Willie cringed, wondering how all that bounty stayed confined inside the elf costume. "I love a Scottish accent."

"British, dear. I'm no a highlander." She deepened her accent, "I'm a sassenach." *The girl watches way too much Outlander.* With a wave, she headed toward the exit.

Tossing her cup into the trash, she met Gator at the door. From the scowl on his face, he definitely wasn't a happy camper.

"What were you doing sitting with Francine Ferguson? That woman is the biggest gossip in five parishes."

"Then I was obviously talking to the right person, wasn't I? Or isn't it my job to find out about Holly Jolly Holiday Helpers?"

"That's not the kind of gossip Francine likes to spread, Mina."

Willie froze, her whole body going on alert. "What did you call me?" She hadn't heard the name in decades. Nobody called her that except John, her late fiancé.

"Mina? Huh, I guess that's what I've been calling you in my head. Everybody calls you Willie, but you're too—feminine—to be Willie. Mina suits you better. If it's a problem…"

"No, it's alright. I just haven't been called that in a very long time."

He smiled, just the barest turning up of his lips, and she felt a tingling warmth spreading through her. It felt kind of nice to have somebody using that nickname again. She didn't have to read anything more into it, did she?

"Back to Francine. She able to tell you anything useful?" Gator's hand reached up, scratching at the fake whiskers, which in turn dislodged the wire-rimmed glasses. Without thinking, she reached and pushed them back up, her fingertips skimming along his cheek.

"Not much, other than she wondered why you were Santa, seeing as how you hate Christmas."

He scowled. "I don't hate Christmas. I just don't make a big deal about it."

Beneath his words lay a quagmire of unanswered questions, but it wasn't any of her business, now was it? *Wilhelmina, old girl, get your mind in the game. You are here for one reason only, finding the flim-flam man and shutting him down. Not to psychoanalyze Gator Boudreau, no matter how much the man fascinates you.*

"We'll need to come up with a good reason for you to be

portraying old Saint Nick. Tell people you're donating your salary to a local shelter or helping homeless vets or something to throw off any suspicion."

"Wouldn't be any suspicion if yapping old busybodies would mind their own business, and keep their noses out of mine."

She wanted to laugh at his disgruntled tone. Too bad, she understood what he felt perfectly well. There's a fine art to being able to blend into the background, where nobody sees you as anything but scenery or stage dressing. Draw too much attention and your cover is blown to pieces.

"The other young lady at the table is Patti. Didn't get a last name, but she is an elf. Shall I give you three guesses which shop she's working at?"

His brows rose along with the corners of his mouth. "Seriously, you've already gotten friendly with somebody at Holly Jolly Holiday Helpers? I'm impressed, Mina."

There it was again, that little zip up her spine at the use of her name. It had to be the novelty of it, nothing more. She'd long ago decided to live out the rest of her life as the proverbial old maid, helping raise Mister Samuel, and hopefully his children, once he and Miss Andrea start having little ones.

"Well, judging by first impressions, I don't believe she's the mastermind of their little scheme." She made a circular motion beside her temple. "I think the hamster wheel is spinning, but nobody's running."

"Ah, gotcha. They didn't hire her for her brains."

"More than likely, it's because she fills out the costume

to a tee." Her hands went to the bottom of her corset, tugging it down again. Darn her big hips. The thing didn't want to sit cinched at her natural waist, instead riding upward and pushing her breasts up and out. Thank goodness she had the white frilly apron on over the dress while she worked, or the kiddies and their parents would get quite a show.

"She might be our ticket in."

"Precisely my thoughts. I think I'll bring a plate of cookies tomorrow. Sharing is caring, after all." She patted his chest, feeling the pillowy stuffing under his jacket. "Time to get back to work. You don't want to disappoint the children, Santa."

Chapter Five

Dressed in dark jeans and a black T-shirt, Gator walked through the employee entrance of The Great Escape, located by the kitchen. Since it wasn't yet dawn, supply trucks were being unloaded, box after box of fresh produce and giant coolers of locally-caught seafood. Nobody noticed one lone man slipping through the propped-open doors. The ball cap shadowing his face helped with anonymity.

Making his way through the kitchen toward the front of The Great Escape, he planned to do a little snooping before the Christmas shops opened for business. Most of them were scheduled to open at nine a.m. While he probably wouldn't be able to get inside, he was willing to gamble one or two would be easy surveillance.

Other than the front desk, most of the first floor was cloaked in semi-darkness. Lights burned low, each storefront's display highlighted by temporarily installed spotlights mounted on the ceiling, ensuring people strolling through after hours might see the cheerful holiday displays, and the goods available for purchase.

Gator knew the drill, one he'd be using for decades. *The key to stealth is to act like you belong. Nobody's gonna stop and ask you any questions if you're part of the scenery.*

A whole lot of people working for the hotel didn't know him, because this wasn't his usual stomping grounds. No, he was more comfortable down on the riverfront, hanging with the down-on-their-luck vets, or going on a run with the shrimpers. Yet, he'd learned to blend into whatever environment he had to, to get the job done. He had the scars to prove it.

Stopping in front of Holly Jolly's door, he studied the festive holiday display. It showcased boxes and bows, packages wrapped with elegant paper and ribbons, everything a bright splash of color against a snowy white picket fence. They even had a huge red felt sack, filled to overflowing with unwrapped toys. A blonde-haired doll, a red fire engine, a video game controller, and a baseball mitt and ball decoratively spilled out the top.

The sign over the door displayed the name of the charity. A huge gift-wrap-covered barrel sat in the hall, ready to be filled with the upcoming day's haul. All-in-all, it looked aboveboard and honest.

Except it doesn't feel right.

He'd called in a favor from an ex-CIA spook, somebody he'd worked with before, who'd run a computer search on the charity. The incorporation papers showed it had been formed less than six months ago. The name of the holding company was squeaky clean, but that didn't mean everybody involved had sterling reputations. His friend agreed to keep digging. Who knows, maybe he'd find something, and Gator would be able to end this case soon.

He needed to get inside, but B&E wasn't his specialty.

As much as he didn't want to, he might have to call in another favor. One that could get him barred from C.S.S. and straight into Samuel's black books.

Was it worth it? Without a doubt, because if he turned a blind eye, he was as culpable as the actual shysters who didn't blink an eye at taking advantage of people who could ill afford to lose everything.

"You should have called me if you'd planned to do a little reconnoissance work. I can be your lookout."

"Dammit, Mina. What are you doing here?"

"Probably the same thing you are. Checking out Holly Jolly Holiday Helpers."

He blew out a deep breath. "On first glance, nothing stands out. But a second set of eyes might see something I've missed. Go ahead," he motioned toward the window. "Tell me what you see."

Mina moved forward, leaning in toward the window display, and peered inside. Bent over slightly at the waist, his eyes zeroed in on her backside. Encased in a pair of dark jeans, he couldn't help noticing what a fine backside it was, too.

"You're right. Everything appears precisely as they claim. A donation drop-off location for toys. There is a sign above the counter. I can't make it out from here, though."

He moved to stand behind her, and she straightened abruptly, bumping against him. Placing a hand on the small of her back, he leaned past her to stare in the window. He could feel the heat of her skin through the thin black sweater she wore.

"I can make out the first line, which says something about cash donations. One of us needs to get in there today, find out what the rest of it says."

Mina nodded. "I can do that during my break. Stop by and chat with Patti."

At the sound of approaching footsteps, he led her away from Holly Jolly's window and toward another, this one filled with a variety of candles. Even through the closed door, he detected the scent of clove, evergreen, and peppermint.

"Morning, folks." The security guard waved, continuing on past them toward the kitchen area.

"Guess he thinks we're guests," she whispered.

"Works for me."

There was an awkward silence that seemed to go on forever. He cleared his throat. "Not much more we can do, at least until the shops open. We're not scheduled until ten a.m. Let's go get some coffee."

At her startled look, he realized his suggestion had come out sounding more like a command. She shook her head and chuckled.

"That's hours away. Why don't we head back to my place? I'll fix us breakfast."

His stomach definitely liked that idea. "Sure it's not too much trouble?"

"Nonsense. I offered. Besides, I'm going to use you as a guinea pig." She grinned, and it lit her whole face. Warmth spread through him.

"Guinea pig?"

"I'm trying out a new recipe. None of my boys have

sampled it yet, so you can be the first. I know you'll be honest and tell me if it's palatable."

"Mina, I don't think you could cook anything that didn't taste delicious." He started toward the kitchen area, but stopped after a few steps. "I'm parked down the street. Came in through the employee entrance. How'd you get in?"

She gave him a seductive little smile, before stepping past him. "A girl's got to have a few secrets. Meet you at my place." Giving him a little wave, she spun around and walked in the opposite direction, leaving him standing with his mouth open—and a whole lot to think about.

Chapter Six

Yanking open the freezer door, Willie grabbed the cinnamon pull-aparts she made a few days earlier, tossing the package on the counter to defrost. She only had a couple of minutes before Gator arrived.

With a self-conscious gesture, she brushed her hands against her hips, frowning at the extra inches stubbornly clinging to her silhouette. Damn and blast. No matter how hard she tried, she couldn't drop those last ten stubborn pounds. Losing the first forty—difficult but doable. Now, the needle on the scale seemed superglued in place, because the darn thing wouldn't budge.

Debating whether she had enough time to change out of the jeans, the knock on the door made the decision for her. Huffing out a short breath, she walked over and pulled the door open.

The way Gator's eyes studied her sent a lightheaded, giddy feeling through her. Nobody had looked at her that way since John died. *What will it hurt, to give in to a little temptation? Nobody will get hurt, or be any the wiser, right?*

Giving her head a shake, she motioned for Gator to enter. He walked across the living area with an easy, prowling gait, his feet silent on the bamboo hardwoods.

Watching him, she had to admit, he looked damned fine both coming and going.

"The oven's preheating. It'll just take a minute, then I can pop in my latest project. Can I get you some coffee? Tea?"

"Coffee, please. Cream, two sugars."

Striding into her kitchen, she felt a mantle of calm envelope her. This was her domain, where she felt comfortable. Feeding people brought her a unique sense of joy. While some might look at that as an old-fashioned trait, she didn't care. She was old school, and when she'd left British Intelligence, cooking and baking had been the one thing that kept her sane—well, that and taking care of the Carpenter family.

Popping a coffee pod into the brewer, she shoved a mug in place. It was one of those novelty-type mugs with sayings on the front. Somehow, she ended up with dozens of them. Over the years, Mister Samuel and Miss Lily had given her a few. Her boys at C.S.S. often gave her ones they'd pick up, saying it reminded them of her. A silly thing really, because she was a tea drinker, yet she treasured each one because they'd been given with love.

"What did you make?" Gator loomed over the edge of the peninsula, eyeing the covered baking dish.

Lifting off the lid, she slid it into the oven, hiding her smile. As much as he tried to be nonchalant about it, Gator always seemed to show up whenever she hand-delivered goodies downstairs.

And he really likes my lemon scones.

"It's a new cinnamon roll recipe, only instead of individual rolls, they are pull-aparts. Shouldn't take long to heat them."

Reaching into the refrigerator, she pulled out a small covered container, and took off the lid. She'd made the cream cheese frosting earlier. Grabbing a spoon, she began swirling it around the gooey depths, whisking it faster and faster as it loosened up. She finished right as the oven timer dinged.

"Perfect timing." Lifting out the hot dish with a potholder, she set it on a trivet and began spooning the frosting on the piping-hot pastry. The aroma of fresh cinnamon and nutmeg wafted in the air, and she bit back a smile at the rumble coning from Gator's stomach.

"That smells so good, it makes your tongue jump up and smack your face."

Willie chuckled at his joke. "I hope so. You get to be the first to try them." Lifting the whole baking dish, along with the trivet, she placed it directly in front of him, and watched him inhale deeply. "Let me get a plate and some napkins."

Turning, she placed a hand against her stomach, trying to hush the quivering butterflies rioting inside. Darn, but she felt like a schoolgirl again around this man.

She handed him a small plate and watched him pull several of the round balls free from the steaming pan, white icing coating his fingertips. Watched him lick the messy sweetness away, and she bit back the urge to place her lips against his, and taste it for herself.

Instead, she watched him pop a golden nugget into his

mouth, the corners of his lips kicking upward as he chewed.

Does he like it? Maybe I screwed up the recipe—he's not saying anything. Why isn't he saying anything?

Without a word, he popped another ball into his mouth, before wiping his lips with the napkin.

"Those are amazing. Makes me wonder why you haven't opened your own bakery. I know a guy, if you're interested."

"Thank you, but no. I do a little baking, dabble mostly, because I enjoy it. And my boys seem to like it. Besides, I'm getting too old—"

"Stop right there." She almost wilted beneath the scowl on his face. "You are not old. You're a beautiful woman in the prime of her life, who can do any damn thing she wants to."

Beautiful? Gator Boudreau thinks I'm beautiful? Her insides did a little happy dance, while her brain absorbed the words, then repeated them in her head. *Gator Boudreau thinks I'm beautiful!*

"I...thank you, Gator."

Reaching forward, his fingers slid across her cheek, before tucking her hair behind her ear. The move wasn't overtly sexual. He never uttered a word, but his gaze darkened with a sensuality Willie couldn't deny. The gesture, simple and sweet, was as intimate as any caress, and her breath caught in her throat, heat spreading across her cheeks.

"We...um...we need to talk about our next step." *Oh, no, did that come out sounding like I meant* our *next step?*

"I've got a call in to the bank. I know…"

"You know a guy?" Willie smiled at the hint of red that

spread across Gator's cheeks. "Is there anybody in New Orleans that you don't know?"

"Well, there is this blonde I'd like to know a whole lot better."

It was her turn to blush, at the implication in his words. Did he really want to see her, maybe get to know each other on a more than professional level? The thought was mind-boggling.

"That might be arranged—once we've caught the bad guys."

"Good." He reached forward and snagged another pull-apart from his plate and popped it into his mouth. His hum of appreciation was music to her ears. "As I started to say, I know a guy at the bank who's checking into Abigail's account, working on finding out why and how her money disappeared from her checking account. He's going to call me as soon as he discovers anything."

"Excellent." Willie wiped her hands along her jean-clad thighs, then stood. "We've got time for another cup of coffee before we head back to Santa's Village."

Gator placed a hand on her arm, and she froze, her eyes glued to his face. That simple touch sent sparks zinging through her.

"I meant what I said. When this is over, I want to get to know you, Wilhelmina McDaniels. There's something between us, and I want to explore it. Find out if this," he motioned his hand between them, "can be more than simple friendship. But tell me now if you're not interested, and I'll back off and never mention it again."

She huffed a short laugh. "Gator, I don't want you to walk away. You're right, there's chemistry between us, something I haven't felt for anybody in a long time. My answer is yes. When this case is finished, let's see where this attraction leads." Drawing in a deep breath, she decided total honesty would be her best bet. "But I have to know—are you ready to move on?"

A pained look crossed his face, there and gone in a split second, but she saw it and her heart sank.

"I loved my wife with all my heart. Miss her every day. But she's been gone a long time, and I'm tired of being alone. If all I wanted was a willing female in my bed, I could get that. I want more—with you."

She studied his face carefully, and read the truth in his words. Deciding to take a chance, she reached forward and cupped his cheek, brushing her thumb against the corner of his lips, felt their softness beneath her touch.

Be bold, Willie. Take a chance and make that leap of faith. You'll either fall or you'll fly. Go for what you want.

Leaning forward and closing the short distance between them, she pressed her lips against his. Felt his shocked intake of breath before he responded, taking control of the kiss. His lips moved against hers, and this kiss felt more right than anything had in a very long time.

Breaking the kiss, she smiled and hoped he didn't notice the slight trembling in her hands.

"Time to get to work. I suddenly have the urge to catch an elf."

Chapter Seven

"I love that you're giving back to all those unfortunate children." Willie picked up a stuffed teddy bear with a bright red ribbon around its neck, sitting atop the pile of donated gifts. "Whose idea was this?"

Patti paused, a piece of tape dangling from her fingers. "I'm really not sure. Hey, I'm just grateful to have a job for the holidays, ya know? It's been a tough year."

"Things have been rough for a lot of folks recently." Trying to be unobtrusive, she looked around the storefront, noting a whole lot more toys than the previous day. Huge clear plastic containers overflowed with unwrapped toys of every kind, while gaily wrapped packages were stacked head high against the walls, ready to be delivered to waiting children on Christmas morning.

She really hoped the charity was legit, and there was some kind of misunderstanding about Gator's friends' money being stolen. Swindled. Yet her realistic side dinged as loud as one of those bells the ringers outside the stores rang, collecting money.

"No matter, it's still a very worthwhile thing. Thinking about kids waking up Christmas morning and there not being any gifts under the tree…"

"Yeah. Some of the shelters don't even have trees, can you believe it? But they're more than happy to get the donations."

She watched as two well-dressed matrons began adding toys to one of the big bins outside the shop's front door, chatting merrily with each other. Looking around again, she performed a rough calculation in her head of the retail cost of the toys. Just the unwrapped ones in the bins had to be in the thousands of dollars. And those were only for the ones she could see.

Apparently Santa's helpers were feeling magnanimous this year, or his elves had been extra busy, because their coffers overflowed. At this rate, not only would Orleans Parish see an abundance of toys donated to homeless and womens' shelters, but they'd have enough to share with surrounding parishes.

"I think I'm going to stop by the shops on the way home, and pick up a few things. You can never have enough toys, can you?" Willie tossed out the words, waiting to see how Patti would respond.

The other woman kept wrapping, smoothing sticky tape over the folded seams of gaily printed paper, before picking up a spool of thin ribbon and running it along the edge of a pair of scissors, creating a massive twist of curls. There was no hiding the fact, she'd done this before—probably hundreds of times.

"I'm sure Holly Jolly appreciates every donation." Pop went her gum, the sound audible over the holiday music pouring out of the overhead speakers.

"Oh, wait, I forgot. I can't get to the shops tonight." Willie decided to play a hunch. "Do you think I could give some money instead?"

Patti's head sprang up at the word money. "We're not allowed to take credit cards. Something about processing fees. When Malcolm talked about it, I kinda tuned him out. But checks are okay, and cash too." She mumbled something unintelligible under her breath that Willie couldn't quite hear, though she didn't sound happy.

"What's wrong with using cretit cards? I'd think that would make things simpler."

"Beats me. You can ask Malcolm the next time he shows up." Patti popped her gum again, and it took every ounce of willpower Willie had not to hold out her hand and tell her to spit it out, just like she'd done with the Carpenter children when they'd been little—before she broke them of the nasty habit of chewing gum at all. "I asked the same thing, and he told me it was something to do with taxes and accountability, some gobbledygook. But then again, I don't deal with the money. I'm simply here to collect toys and wrap them." She shot Willie a grin. "Personally, I'm overqualified for the job, but beggars can't be choosers, and I needed the work."

"A sentiment I understand perfectly. Speaking of, I need to get back to my job, since break time is over. See you later?"

"You bet."

Walking back to Santa's changing cubicle, neatly tucked away from prying eyes, she ducked inside. Gator sat with his back against the wall, legs stretched out, phone to his ear.

When his eyes met hers, he held up a finger in the universal *wait a minute* sign. Not wanting to intrude, she reached for the apron hanging on the hook, right where she'd left it when she'd stepped away. The ties became twisted in her hands, as she reached behind her, and she bit back a curse.

"Lemme help." Gator's voice came from right beside her ear, and she jumped, not having heard him finish his call.

"Thank you. I seem to be all fumble-fingered today."

His hands made quick work of the apron strings, and he stepped away. When she turned and got a good look at his face, she knew whoever he'd been talking to on the phone hadn't imparted good news.

"What's wrong?"

"My contact at the bank hasn't been able to find out a thing about the missing funds. I have a feeling I'm going to have to call in some help on this case. Dammit, I was hoping between the two of us, we could figure things out and put a stop to the scheme before anybody else lost any money."

"What kind of help are you thinking about?"

"Figured I'd talk to Carlisle. See if he can find a pattern or something. Ranger and Jean-Luc swear nobody gets anything past Carlisle's computer skills."

"That's not going to work." Willie reached out and straightened the button that was coming undone on his red Santa jacket. "Mister Stefan is out of town. San Diego, I believe. Mister Samuel insisted he take a mandatory vacation." She couldn't help grinning as she remembered the disgruntled look on the younger man's face when Samuel gave him the ultimatum—either take some time off or he was fired.

"Well, his timing sucks."

"I might be able to help. I'm not too shabby with a computer. Or we could ask Miss Andrea. She's a whiz at hack…I mean doing computer investigation."

Oops, she'd almost said too much. Although Gator Boudreau hung around Carpenter Security and did some unofficial work off the books, he wasn't privy to all the goings on, the inner workings of the elite team. Or maybe he was—all four of his sons worked for C.S.S. Jean-Luc was second-in-command of the security company. He probably didn't keep a lot from his dad.

"Andrea might be a good choice, if she can keep Samuel from wanting to take over. We need to keep our investigation on the down low. This is personal business, not company business. Think she could handle that?"

Willie rolled her eyes and almost snorted a laugh. Andrea was Samuel's fiancée, and the list of things he didn't know about her activities could fill a thousand page tome.

"Let's finish out our shift, and I'll talk to her when I get home. Honestly, I think she'll jump at the chance. She's going a little stir crazy with all the wedding plans."

"Want me to be there when you talk to her?"

"It's not necessary, I can fill her in." Straightening her mobcap, she gave him a grin. "Let's go make some rug-rats day, Santa."

Chapter Eight

The line of children waiting to sit on Santa's lap circled around the entire lobby. Judging from the unhappy looks on the parents' faces, they weren't happy campers either.

Gator patted his knee, and the next little boy scrambled up, and he grunted when he got poked in the ribs with a bony elbow as the kid settled in place.

He was a cute little kid with bright red hair sticking out in every direction beneath a white knit cap, brilliant green eyes, and enough freckles to play connect-the-dots for hours. Couldn't be more than five, he'd guess.

"Ho, ho, ho! Merry Christmas. Santa's been watching. Have you been a good boy this year?"

The tyke shook his head, the most forlorn expression crossing his face Gator had seen in a long time. "No, Santa," he whispered. "I did something really bad. That's why I wanted to see you—to tell you not to bring me any toys for Christmas."

Gator's eyes shot straight to the boy's mother, who stood a few feet away, holding the hand of a tow-headed girl of maybe two or three. The way she chewed her bottom lip, and cast furtive glances his way, she was definitely worried about whatever the little boy had to say.

"Well now, tell Santa all about it and maybe we can fix things."

Again, he shook his head. "Can't fix nothing. Bitsy's dead, and it's all my fault."

Bitsy? Dead?

"Wanna tell Santa what happened to Bitsy?"

The little boy's eyes narrowed. "You're supposed to know everything. How come you're asking me if you already know?"

Gator bit back his grin. *Smart kid.* "Part of making things right is admitting what happened. If you want to fix things, you have to tell the truth."

Down went the kid's head, hanging so low Gator couldn't see his face at all. He could barely hear the whispered, "I didn't mean it," before the kid's shoulders started quivering.

Beside him, Willie leaned over, placing her hand on his shoulder. "Maybe I can take him aside with his mother and sister, while you work the line."

Glancing up, he saw clusters of people in a line snaking across the lobby, waiting for their children's turn to speak to Santa. Heaving out a breath, he nodded.

"I want you to go with Mrs. Claus and sit with her for a few minutes. Take your mom and sister with you, and I'll be over soon. Then we'll talk. Okay, little man?"

The tear-streaked face turned up to his, and he almost caved, ready to leave the rest of the people to rot. This kid was broken up about whatever happened to Bitsy. Remembering his own kids dealing with what he assumed was the death of a pet, the boy needed to let go of the grief, or it would eat him alive. But when you're little—you don't know that.

"Okay, Santa."

Like a little monkey, he clamored off Gator's lap and put his hand in Mina's. It hadn't surprised him one bit that she'd made a fine Mrs. Claus. She was a sweet-hearted woman, and apparently adored children. He watched her walk toward the mother, and he motioned for the next child to climb aboard his lap.

Willie led the little boy and his mother and sister over to wait near Santa's changing area, tucked into a narrow hall between two storefronts.

"What's going on?" The mother looked around, concern etched on her weary face.

"Don't worry, sweetie," Willie whispered. "Santa wants a few minutes with young..." Her words trailed off as she realized she had no clue what the youngster's name was. Somehow, she doubted Gator had a clue either.

"Frankie."

"Am I in trouble?" The words came out on a broken sob, the sound tearing at her heart.

"No, honey, you're not in trouble. Santa obviously thinks you're very special." She knelt down until she was face-to-face with Frankie. Leaning in, she whispered, "Do you see him asking any of the other children to wait for him?" Frankie shook his head. "No, because he wants to talk to *you*. That means you're special. You and your sister."

Reaching into her apron, she pulled out the bag of cookies she'd brought with her, thinking to give Gator a little treat during his break. It looked like Frankie and his sister needed them more.

"I made these this morning. Fresh from the North Pole. Think you could eat one?"

He shook his head. "Give it to Hannah."

"Well, I have one right here for Hannah. And one for your mom, too. But this one is just for you." She pressed the chocolate chip cookie into his hand, and passed the bag to his mother with a wink.

Taking a bite, his eyes widened. He must have tasted the surprise she'd added to this batch. In addition to chocolate chips, she'd also added some chocolate-covered raisins.

"It's good," he said around a mouthful of crumbs. "Mom, you gotta try it."

Willie watched the three munch away at their treat, before her eyes instinctively sought out Gator. The line had dwindled down to just a handful. Hopefully, they'd be quick, because she had a feeling Frankie had some major guilt that needed assuaging pronto.

After another cookie had been consumed by each, Gator finally put the closed sign in front of Santa's gilt chair and headed toward their little group.

"Santa, Frankie and Hannah waited, like you requested." Willie's hand rested on the little boy's shoulder, and she felt his body stiffen at Gator's approach. Whatever the child wanted to say had him terrified, and she was having no part of that. Kids needed to know they were loved and cherished, not scared half out of their wits.

"Indeed, Mrs. Claus. I see you gave them some of my cookies." His brow arched and she chuckled.

"Well, Mr. Claus, they looked like they needed them more than you, so I gave them *all* the cookies."

All of them? he mouthed, a pained look above his fake beard. Willie bit the inside of her cheek to keep for chuckling at his disappointed look.

"Don't worry, dear, I'll make a fresh batch when we get back to the North Pole."

With a shake of his head, he knelt beside Frankie, bringing him down to the little guy's level. *Good move, Gator.*

"Frankie, you started to tell me about Bitsy. What happened?" He watched Hannah bury her face against her mother's hip, her tiny arms wrapped around her thigh.

"It was an accident. I didn't mean it, but I ran outside, and the door didn't shut all the way, and Bitsy got out, and got kilt." Frankie's words ran together into one long sentence, getting faster and faster until at the end he was out of breath.

Willie's heart clenched at his mournful expression, and she held her breath, waiting to see what Gator would do.

"Tell me about Bitsy. What did she look like?" Gator tugged off one of the mittens and shoved it into his pocket, and Willie watched him place his large hand on Frankie's shoulder.

"Bitsy is—was—our dog. She was a dack, um, duck

something."

"Dachshund."

"Yeah. A weiner dog. I didn't mean for her to get kilt, Mr. Santa. I chased her, trying to catch up, but she ran into the street, and…"

Willie's stomach knotted, because she knew exactly how the story ended. There was no happy way to fix this.

"Because Bitsy got killed, you think you're on the naughty list?" Gator's eyes met hers over the top of Frankie's head.

Frankie nodded. "I am on the naughty list. I wasn't supposed to go outside, but I wanted to play. If I hadn't been bad, Bitsy wouldn't have got hit by the car."

With the sinewy strength of a jungle cat, Gator slid the rest of the way to the floor, sitting with his legs folded, and pulled Frankie onto his knee.

"Kiddo, did you deliberately leave the door open because you wanted Bitsy to get hurt?"

Frankie adamantly shook his head.

"Did you deliberately lead Bitsy into the street, hoping for a car to come and hit her?"

Again another vehement head shake. "Course not."

"Then what happened was an accident. You didn't do anything on purpose to make Bitsy get hit. Were you careless? Yes. And a bad thing happened, but that doesn't make you a bad or naughty boy. I only have one question, and I want you to tell me the whole truth. Can you do that?"

"Yes, sir."

"Okay, look me in the eyes and answer this one question." Gator paused a long moment. "Are you sorry?"

"Yes."

"Then you're not on the naughty list. Now, I want you to tell me the one thing you want for Christmas, the most important thing you can think of—can you do that?"

Frankie looked at Gator, his eyes huge in his still-pale face. Willie was afraid he wouldn't answer. Finally, he leaned forward and cupped his hand around Gator's ear and whispered. Gator nodded and whispered something back, and she watched the most beautiful smile cross the little boy's cheeks, warmth spreading through her until she felt all tingly inside.

Frankie climbed off Gator's lap, and raced over to his mom, throwing his arms around her waist and hugging her tight. With a smile and a wink, Gator crooked his finger at Hannah, who gave him a sideways look before burying her face against her mother's legs.

"Hannah, you need to tell me what you want for Christmas, so I can make sure the elves make it special just for you."

Her eyes widened and she raced over to perch on Santa's knee, and began spewing forth her extensive list. Willie walked over and placed her hand on the mother's arm.

"Everything's gonna be fine, dear. You wait and see."

"Thank you both. Frankie's been eaten up with guilt, and nothing I said could make him forgive himself. Seeing him smile again, well, that's my very own Christmas miracle."

Willie watched Gator, with his fake fluffy white beard and red Santa hat cocked jauntily on his head, and wondered if she wasn't watching her own Christmas miracle.

Chapter Nine

Willie opened her apartment door at the first knock. She'd been expecting Andrea to show up any moment. When Gator first asked her to help with his friends' dilemma, knowing she wouldn't be around C.S.S. as much as they were used to, she confided in Andrea about working on the little project with Gator.

Andrea's face broke into a huge grin. "So, tell me everything."

Heat flooded her cheeks at the younger woman's words. "Not much to tell yet. Though I do believe Mr. Boudreau is correct, something is off about Holly Jolly Holiday Helpers. I haven't been able to dig deep enough yet—but I will."

"I have no doubt." Sauntering across the living room, Andrea plopped down into one of the two overstuffed chairs situated in front of the fireplace. Willie loved the cozy, intimate look of the space. It was the perfect place for a nice cup of tea in the evenings. She'd decorated the space to feel comfortable and homey, rather than going for any kind of formal elegance. She'd had enough of that in Dallas. Mister Samuel's home had been lovely, and there were times when she missed the extravagance and decadence of the mansion. Yet this small apartment suited her tastes, and she'd come to love her new home.

"I should warn you," Andrea crossed her legs and leaned back in the chair, "Samuel's starting to get antsy. Some of the guys noticed you haven't been around. And before you ask, no, I didn't tell him what you're up to. Between you and me, I think they miss all the treats you bring them."

"Oh, dear. I never meant you couldn't tell him."

"Ms. Willie, we both know what will happen if Samuel gets wind of what's going on. He'll steamroller his way right into the middle of things and take over."

Willie knew Andrea was right. It was the reason she hadn't told him in the first place. Well, that and Gator had asked for her help, because he wanted to keep things close to the vest.

"Anyway, tell me what you've found so far."

"That's my problem, dear. I haven't found anything. Though it's only been a few days. I've cozied up to one of the elves who works for Holly Jolly's. A bit of a ditz, but sweet."

"Sounds like a good start."

"I've gotten into the front of their shop and looked around, but everything seems on the up and up. They are collecting unwrapped toys and monetary donations. Patti, that's the young lady I was telling you about, wraps them, and gets them ready for delivery."

"Is there any kind of checklists of the donations, some kind of recordkeeping? Since it's a charity or nonprofit, they're bound to have meticulous recordkeeping."

Willie smiled. Miss Andrea had a sharp mind. She liked

that, because she'd need it to keep up with Mister Samuel. But it also worked for her in this instance, because she was a problem solver, finding patterns and solutions others didn't spot.

"Precisely why I wanted to talk with you."

Andrea leaned forward in the chair, resting her elbows atop her knees, a curious twinkle in her eyes. "Anything you need, I'm in."

"I was wondering if you might utilize your computer skills, and see what you can find out about Holly Jolly Holiday Helpers."

"Wouldn't you rather ask Carlisle?"

"Mister Stefan has his hands full at the moment, what with Mister Samuel making him take a vacation." She leaned forward and spoke *sotto voce*. "I believe he's gone to see Savannah."

Andrea giggled. "Yep, he's in San Diego right now. About time, if you ask me. He's been pining over her for months."

She understood more than Andrea knew about his infatuation. There had been more than one late night where she'd smuggled a few cupcakes or cookies down to Mister Stefan's place, and they'd talked. He might not be ready to voice his feelings about Savannah, and he was already halfway head-over-heels about her, but he was smart enough to know that poor girl needed time to deal with the horrific ordeal she'd been through.

"Since he's on vacation, and this is such a small thing, I thought maybe…"

"I'll do it," Andrea interrupted. "Lemme run upstairs and grab my laptop, and I'll be right back."

Before Willie could protest and say it could wait until morning, Andrea was out the door.

"Guess I'd better put on some tea."

"Okay, let me take a peek at who's behind our little charity." Andrea began typing, and Willie stood behind her, watching. While she could make her way around a computer, even do a little basic cyber-snooping of her own, she didn't have the skills Andrea had developed over her years working as a CIA agent. Her own MI-5 training had been more face-to-face information acquisition, something she'd excelled at.

"That's interesting."

"What?"

"Holly Jolly Holiday Helpers has only been in existence for about six months. That might not raise a lot of red flags on its own, because new charities start up all the time."

"But..." Willie encouraged her to go on.

"The name of the owner is listed as Kristofer Nicholas." Andrea's eyes met hers. "Seems a little bit too Santa oriented, wouldn't you say?"

"It could be legitimate—if the parents really had it in for their child and gave them such an awful name—but my old investigative senses all say I don't think so."

"Yeah, me neither." Andrea turned back to the computer screen. "Let's do a little checking on Mr. Nicholas, shall we?" Her fingers flew across the keys, and page after page popped up on the screen.

"Hmm." She pointed to one page displayed. "Looks like Kristofer Nicholas is registered as a DBA. So let's do a little more digging."

Willie made her way back to the kitchen, knowing Andrea wouldn't come up for air until she'd uncovered every bit of information related to Holly Jolly. She pulled the tea towel off the dough she'd left to rise and checked the springy texture. It was ready to go into the oven.

She slid the four loaf pans into the preheated oven, and set the timer. She was trying another new recipe, this one for a sweet wheat bread for sandwiches, similar to Hawaiian bread, but with a little heartier texture. Soon the room was filled with the fragrance of baking bread.

"Son of a ..."

"Find something?"

"Yeah, but not what I was expecting." Andrea stood and stretched, arching her back. "Hey, what smells so good?"

"Bread." Willie knew she needed to redirect Andrea back to the task at hand. "What did you find about Holly Jolly Holiday Helpers?"

"Somebody's running a scam all right, but not the one Gator thinks. Or maybe this is in addition to stealing his neighbor's money. I'll check further into the little old ladies' accounts, but this is something else entirely."

Willie wanted to reach over and shake Andrea, get her to spit out what she knew, instead taking a deep breath. "What else are they up to?"

"Somebody's selling the toys."

Willie's heart squeezed in her chest. *Selling the toys? The ones supposed to go to little kids, babies like Frankie and Hannah? Oh, hell no.*

"How can you tell?"

"A lot of them are listed on sites like Ebay, Craigslist, and a bunch of others. Multiple listings under multiple sellers, but the shipping information is the same for every single entry. And there are hundreds of items for sale. Even if they end up selling them for less than retail, it adds up to a huge chunk of change. And that's only for the ones listed. How many more could have been donated in the last day or so that aren't up on the sites yet?"

"That's not proof. Maybe somebody got a good deal on a bunch of toys and is selling them to make holiday money. Can we prove that it's Holly Jolly?"

"I'm gonna keep digging. I hate to say this, but it makes a kind of twisted logic. Some sleazebag makes a killing selling thousands of dollars of donated toys. Closes up shop and disappears with a pocketful of cash. The phony company is never heard of again, so even if the authorities investigate the fraud, they hit a stone wall. Leaving this perp or perps, since it probably takes more than one lousy jerk working in cahoots, free to scamper off to another town, and do it or a similar version of the scam all over again. It's sad but all too common."

"And the underprivileged children in the shelters get nothing for Christmas." No, this was unacceptable. It was one thing for somebody to pull a confidence scheme on a couple of old ladies, but this was going too far.

"Andrea, dear, keep digging. I need to make some calls." Already Willie could feel her blood pressure rising at the damned injustice. This might have started out as a simple enough operation, skimming a little extra money from donations. But stealing toys from children? No way in Hades was she going to stand by and let that happen.

Picking up her phone, she dialed Gator's number. It rang over and over, finally clicking to voice mail.

"Mr. Boudreau—Gator, it's…Mina." She still couldn't quite wrap her head around the fact he'd begun calling her by the shortened version of her name. She'd expected him to fall in line with everybody else, calling her Willie. After all these years, she'd grown accustomed to the Americanized version of her first name. She still got a catch in the back of her throat at hearing Mina. Nobody had called her that in such a long time—and if she was being honest, she got a tiny thrill he wanted to stand apart from the rest of the C.S.S. team.

"I've got Andrea at my apartment, doing a little computer sleuthing, and she's come up with a cracker of a theory. Please call me when you have a moment, if you wouldn't mind. I'd like to give you a bit of an update. Um, good-bye."

Hanging up, she waved a hand in front of her face, feeling the heat rising in her cheeks. This was bloody ridiculous. She was too old for this sort of foolishness. Stiffening her spine, she dialed another number, one she knew by heart.

"Hello." The soft Texas twang sounded all-too-familiar, and brought a smile to her lips.

"Mister Dean, how are you?"

"Much better now that I've heard your beautiful voice, Ms. Willie. When are you going to leave my no-good brother and run away with me?"

She laughed, because he asked the same question every time they spoke. And she always gave the same answer. "I don't believe hell has frozen over yet, so the answer is not today. Are you busy? I hope I'm not interrupting."

"Nonsense, darlin'. I'm never too busy for you. Whatcha need?"

She could picture him, sprawled out on the massive black leather sofa he insisted on keeping in his living room, though the thing had definitely seen better days. His booted feet, shod in a pair of well-worn cowboy boots, would be propped up on the old Army chest he insisted made a great coffee table. While he might have money, he didn't splash it around in a gaudy show of excess. He'd grown up with humble roots, and didn't ask for a hand out—not from anybody. Few people knew he was Samuel Carpenter's illegitimate brother, a by-product of their father's profligate ways. Ms. Willie did everything she could to let him know he was a welcome part of her life.

"Are you in Austin?"

There was a long pause before he answered. "Actually, I'm not."

"Oh, well…"

She stopped at a knock on her door. "Can you hold on a minute, dear?"

Swinging the door open, she gave a squeal of delight as Dean winked at her. "Told ya I wasn't in Austin."

"I'm so glad you're here."

"Me, too." Andrea walked up behind Willie and grinned at her future brother-in-law. "Did Samuel call you with an assignment," she asked, hugging him.

"I'm like a bad penny, turning up when you least expect me." He tossed his cowboy hat onto the console table beside the door with practiced ease. "Sounds like y'all are up to something—maybe something you don't want big brother sticking his nose into?"

She looked at Andrea, who rocked back on her heels, whistling and staring at the ceiling, refusing to meet Dean's eyes. He laughed aloud at Andrea's display of innocence.

"Okay, what are you beautiful ladies up to?"

Willie grinned at Andrea, whose innocent expression had been replaced with a mischievous smirk. It appeared she wouldn't mind bringing Dean into their little game of *catch the con man*.

"Well, Mister Dean, it's like this…"

Chapter Ten

Dean Westin walked around the lobby of The Great Escape, studying the displays in a casual fashion, watching the employees wander around in their holiday costumes. It was an extravaganza of reds, greens, and golds. Though there were still a couple of weeks before Christmas, people here seemed to embrace the festivity of the season wholeheartedly.

Remaining several feet away from Holly Jolly's shop, which he'd been surveilling for the last thirty minutes, he watched the pile of toys grow, as families dropped off their donations. A pretty blonde in a figure-hugging elf costume dragged the bin inside, before putting an empty one in its place beside the front door. She must be Patti, the girl Ms. Willie told him about, also known as his current mark.

Tossing aside the half-empty cup of hot cocoa, he headed for Holly Jolly's storefront. Christmas music poured from overhead speakers, adding another layer of holiday cheer. Damn, he liked the holidays as much as the next guy, but he'd be stuffing his ears with cotton-balls after about half an hour of that nonstop jolliness.

With a surreptitious glance through the frost-edged windowpane, he spotted the pretty blonde busily giftwrapping a board game. Otherwise, the interior of the shop stood empty. He'd been watching for the last thirty minutes or so, and rarely did anybody go inside; simply adding toys into the collection bin and heading on to other stores, ready to fritter away more of their hard-earned dollars on stuff nobody really wanted.

He strolled inside, shooting a bright smile toward the perky blonde. Yep, her nametag read *Elf Patti* in glittery red letters.

"Morning, ma'am." He tipped the brim of his cowboy hat, and stepped a little closer to her table. "Looks like y'all have gotten quite a haul for the kids."

"It's amazing, isn't it? People have been so generous." She shot him a look he was all too familiar with, starting at the top of his head, and moving downward, before slowly heading back north. He'd deliberately dressed down, wearing old faded jeans, his favorite cowboy boots, and a black pullover sweater, since it had been in the mid-thirties when he'd headed out that morning. Her smile dimmed the tiniest bit, and he knew precisely what she saw when she looked at him. What he'd wanted her to see—a down-on-his-luck cowboy without two nickels to rub together.

Wouldn't she be surprised if she knew my real net worth? Appearances can be deceiving, after all.

"Well, now, I'd like to add a little to that generosity, in the spirit of the season. Just got my Christmas bonus, and thought I'd donate a hefty chunk of it to a worthy cause. And you definitely look like a worthy cause, darlin'."

The blonde blushed at the double entendre, and ducked

her head. Hmm, that was interesting. He'd have expected her to have a ready comeback.

"Holly Jolly Holiday Helpers appreciates your generosity, sir." She slapped another piece of tape onto the wrapping paper, and hastily added a premade bow. Her movements spoke volumes. Miss Patti seemed a tad pissed at his sexual innuendo. *Interesting.*

"Can I make a donation?" He pulled out a roll of bills, making sure Patti saw the Benjamins wrapped around the wad.

"A cash donation? Sure, I can do that. We accept cash and checks."

"I guess it's a good thing I cashed my paycheck, with that nice Christmas bonus then." When her eyes met his, he saw precisely what he expected, a touch of avarice and greed.

"It'll definitely make a difference with the number of toys we can buy for the kids." She leaned forward conspiratorially, making sure he got a good look at her not-so-hidden goodies. "To be honest, cash donations work best because—just between you and me—sometimes the checks bounce."

He shook his head, doing his best to put a mournful expression on his face, and hoping like heck she bought it. "That's a downright shame. I'm only in town for a couple of days, so I've been pretty much operating on a cash basis, since I didn't bring my checkbook. I've got my company credit card, and I can't put a donation on that—my boss would kill me."

Yeah, right, like Samuel would say anything. One good thing about his big brother, he'd given him *carte blanche* when it came to expenses.

"Oh." She looked confused for a moment, then brightened. "I know Holly Jolly Holiday Helpers appreciates you giving so selflessly to help the needy children around New Orleans. So do I."

"I think it's a great thing Holly Jolly Holiday Helpers is doing," he leaned forward and made a show of looking at her name tag before adding, "Patti."

"How much were you thinking about donating, Mister…"

"Dean. Call me Dean, darlin'." He peeled off two hundred dollar bills before pausing, baiting the hook a little more, then adding another. "I can't resist giving to kids. Just love 'em."

She eyed the money for a long moment, before glancing around. "If you can hang on a second, I'll get my receipt book from the back. You know, for your taxes."

"Take your time, sugar. I've got all day." He winked, watching a flush of pink stain her cheeks. "I'm not going anywhere."

With a quick glance toward the door, Patti dashed into the office behind her gift-wrapping station, and Dean turned around, taking a visual inventory of the toys stacked along the shelves. Be a damned shame if what Ms. Willie and Andrea suspected was true. These toys needed to get to children who needed them the most, and if he had any say in it, they'd be under the trees on Christmas morning at the shelters.

At the sound of the door closing behind him, he turned

back around and noted the receipt pad in Patti's hand. Maybe she was on the up-and-up, and really would put the marked bills into the charity's coffers. He hated to be so cynical, but working for Carpenter Security had shown him too much of the ugliness of people, and not a whole lot of good. Still, he'd give her the benefit of the doubt—unless or until she proved him wrong.

"Let's get this done." He watched as she painstakingly wrote out a receipt, noting the charity's name and the donation amount on the page. *So far, so good.*

"Here you go." He laid the bills on the counter, and she snapped them up, placing them inside the front of the receipt pad and handed him his copy.

"You've done a very nice thing here, Dean. I'm sure this will buy a lot of toys, and bring smiles to the kids' faces on Christmas morning."

"That's why we're doing this, right?" Touching the brim of his hat in parting, he turned toward the door.

"Um, Dean?"

"Yes, darlin'?"

"Would you like to maybe go to dinner or something?"

"Wish I could, but I've gotta finish up the job I'm working and head on home to Texas. Appreciate the offer though, Patti." Without a backward glance, he strode from the shop and out into the lobby.

Ms. Willie and Andrea stood beside the front door of the coffee place, Styrofoam cups in their hands. And didn't Ms. Willie look adorable in her Mrs. Claus getup, with her mobcap and corset? She'd dropped a bit of weight since moving to New Orleans, and he couldn't help noticing the side glances she got from a few of the men walking past.

With a nod, he gave the women a quick tip of his hat before heading out, knowing he'd meet up with them later.

Right now, he had a meeting with big brother, to fill him in on the current case he was working. He didn't think big brother was going to be happy with what he'd found.

Chapter Eleven

Gator scratched his stomach, and couldn't help wishing, not for the first time, he'd never heard of Holly Jolly Holiday Helpers. Playing Santa wasn't the worst thing he'd ever done—not by a long shot. He'd survived the Vietcong when he was still a wet-behind-the-ears grunt serving Uncle Sam. He'd raised four hell-raising boys and one girl who could outrun, outshoot, and out cuss any one of her brothers. And he'd survived the death of his beloved Elizabeth. But, dang if this stupid red outfit wasn't getting the best of him. It itched. Constantly. Incessantly. Try not letting the kids feel you squirming in your chair, trying to scratch without tossing them off his lap. Wasn't easy.

Between the itchy red menace of a suit and the fluctuating temperature, he was in holiday hell. The only good part was the kids. Talking to them. Looking at those little faces so filled with wonder and the anticipation of all their dreams coming true. It was like holding his own little ones again.

He smirked at the image of one of his grown sons plopping down on his knee, and telling their Christmas wishes to old Saint Nick. Ranger's would be easy. He just wanted a healthy son or daughter—they'd decided not to find out the baby's gender and enjoy the surprise. Though Gator was pretty sure he knew. Still, he'd refrain from confirming his suspicion, which if he really wanted to know wouldn't take much effort, and enjoy the prospect of being a first-time grandpa.

"There you are." Mina sounded out of breath, and when he looked, her face was flushed the prettiest shade of pink. Little wisps of gold and blonde hair peaked from beneath her cap, and she was putting on the wire-rimmed glasses that completed her outfit. He'd be hard-pressed to think of any other Mrs. Claus looking quite as sexy as the beauty standing in front of him.

"Sorry I didn't get back to you yesterday." He tried adjusting the long-sleeved shirt he wore beneath the jacket. The infernal itching was driving him insane. "Had to take care of a problem, and had my phone turned off."

"I understand, but we've got a bit of news."

"We?"

She ducked her head, not quite meeting his eyes, and got a sinking feeling in the pit of his stomach.

"You knew I was going to ask Ms. Andrea to look into things, as she's quite adept with a laptop."

True. The woman was ex-Agency, so she had a more-than-adequate skill set when it came to computer linguistics. And she'd learned a thing or two from her stepbrother, who'd been her handler, and a force to be reckoned with in his own right.

"She find anything?"

"It looks as if a good portion of the donated toys are being sold online."

"Son of a …" He cut off the expletive, though he noticed Mina nodding her head in agreement. "Is she sure the toys are coming from the charity?"

"She's fairly certain, but is doing some more digging this morning."

A timid knock on the door caused Gator's gaze to swing toward the opening. His neighbor, Abigail Benedict, stood framed in the opening, her handbag clenched tightly in her grip.

"Gator, can I talk to you?" He watched her eyes fasten on Mina, garbed head to toe in her Mrs. Claus outfit. "Alone."

"Abigail, come in. Meet Wilhelmina McDaniels. She's a friend who's helping me look into your problem."

Color washed into the older woman's cheeks before she took a step forward, hand extended. "How do you do, Mrs. McDaniels. It's a pleasure to meet you."

"Please, call me Willie. Everybody does," she added with a sideways glance at him, and he grinned. He'd figured out early on calling her Mina always brought the prettiest blush to her cheeks, but really—there wasn't a woman alive who looked less like a Willie. And Wilhelmina was a mouthful, where Mina rolled off his tongue like a caress.

"Then you must call me Abigail."

The changing space was a little claustrophobic for three people, but they managed, Gator giving up his seat to Abigail.

"I was wondering if you've been able to find out anything about our money? I told the others I'd ask you if there's anything to report."

"Abigail," Mina moved to sit beside his elderly neighbor, and clasped her hand, offering her comfort, "Gator's investigating, and he's brought in a computer expert to dig into Holly Jolly. We want to make sure you and your friends get your money returned. Don't worry, Gator's the best. If anybody can solve this mystery, it's him."

Something inside him warmed at her praise. Though he knew she was only encouraging Abigail, knowing she had faith in him brought forth so many unfamiliar feelings. He didn't feel emotions. He'd shut everything down, been frozen inside since Elizabeth passed. Yet this slip of a woman, with her sweet British accent and her bewitching blue eyes, had his senses spinning.

"Oh, I trust Gator one hundred percent. When I realized what was happening, he was the only person I thought of who'd know exactly what to do." Abigail beamed at him. "I also came because I remembered something. About the man who came to my house."

Gator perked up at her words, his attention riveted. *Now we're talking—give me something to work with.*

"What do you remember, Abigail?" Gator kept his voice low and soothing. From past experience, he knew she became flustered if rushed or pressed. Sometimes it took forever to finally get to the point—though she got there eventually—she always did.

"Well, you know I told you he was dressed like Santa's elf?" Looking at him she chuckled. "Or maybe I should say one of *your* elves." Her comment made him remember the damned itchy red suit, and he deliberately shoved his hand behind his back to keep from scratching.

"Abigail, what did you remember, about the elf?" Bless Mina for getting the older woman refocused. He had that antsy feeling in the pit of his gut, that sixth sense telling him things were about to explode.

"I really don't know why I didn't think of it at the time, but he sneezed."

He tilted his head back and closed his eyes. This was the big revelation? Elfie had allergies?

"Sneezed? Did he have a cold?" Mina asked.

"Oh, no. He said it was allergies. To my precious Muffin. Can you believe that?"

Mina turned a baffled look on him, a question in her gaze.

"Muffin is her cat."

"Ah."

"He sneezed and sneezed, continuously. That's why he left so abruptly, and didn't wait for me to write the check, telling me to bring it by—well, here."

"Abigail, may I try a little experiment with you? It's a game I used to play to help my memory."

Abigail stared at Mina, and he could practically read her confusion and distrust, though she finally acquiesced. "I guess."

Mina glanced his way one more time before pulling her hand free from Abigail's. "Close your eyes, and clear your mind. Don't think about anything. Not about Muffin or Gator or even the elf."

"Sure." Abigail obeyed, her eyelids fluttering closed, her

expression blanking. Gator wanted to chuckle, because it was an expression he was used to seeing on the woman's face. He'd never played poker with her, her face was too open and honest—he'd have cleaned her out in a heartbeat.

"Perfect." Willie claimed. "What's the first color that comes to mind when I say ocean?"

"Blue."

"Very good." Mina kept her voice pitched low and neutral, her British accent disappearing completely as she slid into the Texas drawl she'd affected for so many years. Gator couldn't help smiling at the subtle change in tone and cadence. Abigail hadn't even noticed the difference. But he noticed. He was attuned to every little nuance when it came to the lovely Brit.

"What color is Muffin's fur?"

"Orange."

"Excellent. What color is Gator's coat."

Abigail giggled before answering, "Red."

"Right you are. What color were the elf's eyes?"

"Brown." Abigail's own eyes popped open at her answer. "Oh my goodness, that's right. He had brown eyes."

Mina grinned. "See, you remember more than you think. Care to keep going?" At Abigail's eager nod, she continued. "Close your eyes again, and don't try to focus on anything. Remember, just relax."

Gator watched, mesmerized as Mina grilled Abigail with the skill and finesse of a professional interrogator. His eyes narrowed. There was definitely more to his temporary partner's background than he knew.

"Abigail, what color is a candy cane?"

"Red and white."

"Excellent. What color was the elf's outfit?"

"Green, but he wore ugly shoes."

"Ugly shoes? What do you mean?"

"They didn't match with his outfit. They were black, with tassels on them. Loafers. He wore loafers instead of those cute curled up toe shoes elves wear."

Mina looked at him, and he motioned for her to keep going. Glancing out through the door, he noted a line forming at the Santa booth, but they still had a few minutes before going on shift. Any information they gleaned from Abigail before then was good.

"Okay, Abigail, one more question and we're done. The elf wore a green outfit and ugly black shoes, which didn't match. Picture his outfit in your mind, from his feet to his head. Can you see it?"

"Um, yes."

"Good. What color is his hair?"

"Dark brown—wait—no, that's right. Dark brown. Longer over his ears."

Abigail opened her eyes, staring at Mina. "Did I help?"

Mina leaned over and hugged her. "You most definitely helped. We've got a much better idea of who we're looking for now."

He couldn't help noticing that as soon as Mina was done with her questions, she slipped right back into her British persona, like pulling on a familiar sweater.

"Thank you, Abigail, for stopping by, but it looks like

the kids are waiting for Santa. We're going to have to go." He gave her a warm smile, because he really did care about his neighbor and friend.

"Already?" Mina raced over and snatched her apron off the hook, wrapping the strings around her waist and tying it with a big bow in the back. *Right above that pretty backside of hers.* Gator swallowed past the lump in his throat. He had to stop thinking about Mina in any way except professionally. They were a team, albeit only temporarily, until they'd figured out what kind of scam Holly Jolly was pulling.

Yeah, right. And I need to get my head examined if I convince myself I can go back to just being Mina's friend.

"Mrs. Claus, don't forget the list. We've got to check it twice." He gave her a wink. "Abigail, I'll call you with any news. But, right now, it's show time."

Grabbing hold of Mina's hand, he gave it a squeeze and headed toward the swarm of happy kids.

Chapter Twelve

The next morning, Mina slipped behind one of the large decorated topiaries covered with poinsettias positioned by the corner of the lobby. Her prey lingered several feet away, and so far hadn't spotted her. Dark brown hair, covered with a green felt hat, he barely topped out at five foot five, and only then if she was being generous. The holly green outfit marked him as an employee of one of the Santa's Village shops, but so far he hadn't made it inside any of them.

Instead, he'd stood in the lobby talking on his phone, a marked scowl on his decidedly uncheerful face. There was one thing that made him stand out from the rest of the holiday employees—and drew her immediate attention—his shoes.

The exact ones Abigail described when Mina had questioned her. Black loafers with tassels. Probably wouldn't be out of place in a boardroom filled with executives, dressed in their Georgio Armani and Hugo Boss suits. But paired with an elf's jacket, short pants and tights—something was definitely wrong with this picture.

Too bad she couldn't get closer. She'd love to eavesdrop on whatever put the murderous expression on his ugly mug.

As though he sensed somebody watching, he began surveying the crowd, and she knew she had to move along, or he'd spot her for sure.

Running her sweaty palms against the front of her impeccable white apron, she meandered around the flowering plant and walked toward Holly Jolly's shop. Somehow, her gut instinct screamed he'd be showing up there before too much longer.

Once through the doorway, she looked around, shaking her head at the stacks of toys. There were definitely far fewer than there had been the previous day. Of course, they might have moved them to a warehouse or someplace secure, because the shops in the Santa's Village weren't exactly massive. But, she had a feeling if she went online, she'd find another batch of brand new toys for sale.

"Willie! Is it break time already?" Patti dashed around the counter, her svelte body encased in another costume that made the most of her abundant assets, this one a brilliant crimson red. Over her shoulder, she yelled, "Velma, I'm taking my break. Back in 15."

"I got ya covered." A middle-aged woman with salt and pepper hair sauntered out of the back room, and scooted up onto the stool Patti had abandoned, and started decorating the half-finished present. "I'll hold down the fort. Plus, Malcolm should be in any minute."

Patti's face scrunched up, and she made a hurry up motion toward Willie. "Let's get out of here, before Malcolm shows up."

"Who's Malcolm? I don't think I've met him." Mina's

nose crinkled as she went through the list of people she'd seen working at Holly Jolly.

"Malcolm is the boss. Pushy jerk. Thank goodness he's rarely on site. Something about him gives me the heebie-jeebies."

"Really? You'll have to point him out, so I can avoid him."

"Shoot, hopefully he'll be in and gone before I get back. He rarely hangs around the shop. He's much better about working in the field. Mostly he deals with Velma—she keeps the records and receipts. He collects all the monetary donations, which is why he's coming—so he can take the cash and checks to the bank. The shop is basically just the drop-off place for the folks who want to bring the toys themselves."

Willie's mind raced, cataloging the information Patti unwittingly provided. At last it looked like they might have a name. Maybe Gator could check with Abigail and see if it sounded familiar.

"Oh, crud. There he is." Patti sidled up to Willie, half-hidden from view. She pointed toward the man Willie had spotted earlier. "That's Malcolm."

While the women watched, he stalked through the doors of Holly Jolly's, his bearing rigid and his face a frozen mask.

"Gee, what crawled up his knickers and croaked?"

Patti giggled so hard she snorted. "Willie, I love the way you talk. I swear, that describes Malcolm perfectly. I don't think I've ever seen the man smile—not once."

Willie shrugged, giving Patti a wink. "Some people seem

to be perpetually gloomy. One good yank might pull the stick out of his bum, though."

Patti doubled over, holding her side. "Stop, I can't breathe. But you've nailed it. Sure you haven't met him before?"

Willie's eyes slid back toward the entrance to Holly Jolly's. "I'm sure. But I've met a few like him. Braggarts and bullies. Must have a Napoleon complex."

They stood chatting, silhouetted in the shadows, until Patti said she had to get back to work. Willie bade her goodbye and stood in the corner of the lobby with a clear view of Holly Jolly's front door. Malcolm hadn't come out yet, and she hadn't seen hide nor hair of Gator. She'd shown up early, hoping to get a chance to suss out the place before her shift started. When she'd spotted Malcolm, the gut instinct that had served her well when she was with MI-5 kicked in.

Bingo. There was Malcolm, carrying one of those bank money pouches, the kind with the zipper top. He was on the move, walking briskly toward the front doors of The Great Escape.

She barely had a split second to make a decision, and giving in to her gut, she followed him. With a little luck, she'd have some good news to share with Gator.

Chapter Thirteen

Gator looked at his phone. No missed calls. No texts. And no Mina. It wasn't like her not to show up. The woman was a model of efficiency in everything she did.

Yet the changing area stood decidedly empty. Her apron and mobcap, which she hung up each afternoon when she finished her shift. hung forlornly on its solitary hook. Which meant she hadn't been there, because he distinctly remembered her hanging them there the day before.

"Where the hell are you, Mina?"

Tugging his denim jacket closer, he peered across the lobby toward the coffee area, wondering if she'd stopped in for a cup of tea. Still no sign of her. The candy kiosk yielded similar results.

Shaking his head, he took off toward Holly Jolly's shop. Damn, he hoped she hadn't done anything foolish. What was he thinking? Mina wasn't the impulsive sort. She was methodical and logical. Completely different from Elizabeth, the mother of his children and the love of his life. She'd been spontaneous, dropping everything on a whim to play with the kids, or head to town because they wanted chocolate milk instead of white. Thinking about Elizabeth being gone didn't hurt like it used to. He still loved her, he always would, but he was alive and ready to move on. Elizabeth wouldn't want him to spend his life alone. And starting over might well involve a sassy British woman who had more hidden secrets than a crossword puzzle.

Good thing he loved solving puzzles.

He peered through the glass front window of Holly Jolly Holiday Helpers, and spotted a woman who looked vaguely familiar, though it wasn't the young blonde Mina had befriended. This woman was older, dark-haired and much shorter than the blonde.

"Can I help you?"

He spun at the words, frowning at the sight of Mina's friend, A.K.A., the blonde. She'd probably told him the woman's name, but for the life of him he couldn't recall it at the moment.

"Hi. I'm looking for…"

"You're Gator, right?" At his nod, she giggled. "Willie told me about you."

Hmm, exactly what had she said to bring that cheeky smirk to the girl's lips?

"I'm looking for Willie." Ugh, saying that name left a bad taste in his mouth. But blondie would have no idea who he was talking about if he asked for Mina.

"I saw her when I went on break a little while ago, but not since then. Let me check with Velma, maybe she's talked with Willie."

"Velma?"

She nodded. "Velma's the other elf covering the store. Takes care of logging in the incoming toys. Malcolm handles all the money."

Right, two more names to add to the list of people to check out. In the meantime, Mina was still missing, and he was getting that antsy feeling, the one where the little hairs on the back of his neck stood at attention like wooden soldiers lined up for battle.

"Come on, let's check." With a bouncy step, she walked past him into Holly Jolly's shop. Following closely, he took an assessing glance around. As busy as they'd been over the last couple of days, there weren't all that many toys visible.

"Velma? This is Gator. He's one of Santa's helpers this year."

"Hey." Velma never looked up from the paper she was studying. "Cushy job. Santa's got it easy."

"Try wearing that itchy outfit for hours, you wouldn't be complaining about doing paperwork."

"He's looking for Willie—you know, Mrs. Claus? Have you seen her?"

Velma's head came up, and she studied Gator for a long moment before answering the other woman's question. "Not since you went on break with her earlier. Why?"

"Nothing important. I needed to talk to her before our shift started." Gator had no problem lying to the women, though technically it wasn't a lie. He did want to talk with Mina, but not about work. He'd been working up the nerve to ask her out to dinner, maybe on Christmas Eve.

Yet now he couldn't find her, and his intuition was clanging, a persistent ping in his skull. Something wrong, and he had to find her—fast.

"Hey, guys, what's up?

Gator groaned inwardly at the sound of Francine's voice. Listening to her gossip was the last thing he had time for. Finding Willie took precedent over anything.

"Gator! I was so surprised to see you playing Santa this year. And Willie makes such a wonderful Mrs. Claus."

"Thanks. Have you seen Willie this morning?"

Francine nodded. "Sure did. About fifteen minutes ago, maybe. I didn't get a chance to talk to her though, because she was in such a hurry. She hustled out the front door, quick as you please, without so much as a wave."

"She left? Are you sure?"

Francine crossed her arms over her chest and stared at him. "Of course I'm sure. I watched her walk right across the lobby and out the front. Looked like she was in a hurry, too."

"Thanks." With a nod, he started for the door, and Francine latched onto his arm.

"Gator, what's your hurry? I'm sure she'll be back before the kids start showing up. Maybe we could get some coffee?" She blinked at him, batting her mascara-caked lashes. Then her eyes narrowed, and he recognized that salacious glint in them. The barracuda queen was out, looking for some juicy new gossip, because there wasn't anything Francine loved more than sharing every little tidbit with her friends. "Are you and Willie doing more than playing Mr. and Mrs. Claus? Because if you're seeing her…" Her words trailed off, leaving the open-ended question hanging in the air. Three sets of eyes now stared at him.

I don't have time for this. Gotta find Mina.

"You're right, Francine. We're not only playing Mr. and Mrs. Claus, but I'm crazy about the woman. Go ahead and tell all your gossipy cronies. Let 'em know Gator Boudreau is off the market permanently."

He heard the women gasp as he walked away. Dang, but it felt good to stop Francine in her tracks, though he had a feeling Mina might not be happy when she heard about his bald-faced statement.

Too bad. He meant every word. He had every intention of making the sassy Brit his, but first he had to find her.

Pulling out his phone, he checked again. Still no text messages or voice mails. Where the hell was she?

Chapter Fourteen

I t was a good thing Malcolm was walking to wherever he was headed, because if he'd gotten behind the wheel of a car, he'd have sped away before she could hail a cab. As it was, she practically jogged to keep up.

Block after block she trailed behind him, until he rounded a corner and disappeared from view. Racing to catch up, when she turned onto the street, he was gone.

Vanished.

No—he couldn't have disappeared into thin air. She acknowledged she was a step or two slower than she'd like, but he'd been within clear view until he'd…

Gone into the bank. Peering through the front doors, she spotted the green elf jacket waiting in line for the next available teller. She huffed out a ragged breath. *Guess I'm not in as good a shape as I thought, even with the extra pounds gone.*

Opening the front door, she walked inside, fumbling around in her shoulder bag, pretending to look for something, though her attention was razor-focused on Malcolm the Elf. What a silly name for such a sourpuss. He still clutched the money bag he'd picked up at The Great Escape, and hadn't stopped anywhere along the way.

Had she made a mistake? Because so far, nothing he'd

done raised any red flags. Trying to remain inconspicuous, she moved over to one of the tables lining the center of the bank, the ones where they kept blank deposit slips and pens and envelopes. Pretending to fill one out, all the while she kept her eyes glued to Malcolm.

Next in line, a teller motioned for him, and Willie leaned forward, straining to catch sight of the contents of the pouch. The teller pulled the zipper, and…

"Ma'am is there a problem?"

Ah, hell. Busted. Pasting on her sweetest smile, she blinked at the security guard standing beside the table.

"Oh, no. Nothing's wrong. I do apologize." She emphasized the British accent with each word. Wouldn't hurt to let him think she was a dotty old woman from across the pond. "I thought I saw an acquaintance. Silly me, I was looking for my glasses. Need them for distance, you know? She waved toward the line. "But now I can see it wasn't my friend. Sorry to be a bother."

"No bother, ma'am. If you need anything, let one of the tellers know. They'll be happy to assist you." He touched a finger to the corner of his forehead, in a small salute. "Merry Christmas."

"To you, too."

The second his back was turned, she fanned a hand in front of her face. That had been way too close. And she'd missed Malcolm's entire transaction with the bank telle, and he was headed for the front door.

Shoving everything back into her purse willy-nilly, she raced after him. Darn it, now they didn't know if he was behind the money scam on Abigail and her friends, or if he was on the up-and-up.

With barely a split second to make a decision, she hoped she didn't blow their investigation out of the water, but this might be their only chance, and she had to take it.

Reaching forward, she tapped him on the shoulder. "Excuse me, are you Malcolm?"

He stopped and turned around at her question. "Yes, I am. Who are you?"

Meeting his gaze head on, she answered, "My name is Wilhelmina McDaniels, and if you've got a minute, I think you can help me solve a mystery. Are you game?"

The scowl on his face deepened for a moment, before he shrugged.

"Why not?"

Looping her arm through his, she patted his forearm. "Come along. I'll treat you to a hot cocoa and tell you what's been going on at Holly Jolly Holiday Helpers."

An hour later, Gator still hadn't found Mina. She wasn't answering calls or texts, and his emotions vacillated between pissed off and scared out of his wits.

He'd talked to his friend, who didn't mind taking an extra shift in Santa's Village, which freed him up to search for Mina, but he didn't have a clue where to start.

"Gator!"

Whirling at the sound of her voice, he felt a flash of heat flare to life at the sight of her, with her hand on some other man's arm. On closer inspection, the man in question looked suspiciously like Abigail's elf, right down to the ugly black shoes.

How in the hell did she track him down?

"Gator Boudreau, what the hell is going on?"

Yes, now that he'd gotten a good look, he recognized the elf in question, and was pretty damned sure he wasn't robbing little old ladies of their life savings. Malcolm Nicholas might look like a grinch, but he had a heart as big as Texas, and a wallet to match.

"You know Malcolm?" Willie's crestfallen expression nearly had him chuckling. Apparently, she'd wanted to present Abigail's elf with all the fanfare and pomp and circumstances the situation warranted.

"We've met."

Malcolm held out his hand. "Boudreau, Ms. McDaniels and I had a chat about your suspicions.: The semi-permanent scowl returned to his face. "Nobody is stealing money. Every dime that's come in is documented, whether it's cash or check. I'll be more than delighted to open the ledgers to any accountant, if you'd like."

"Not necessary, Malcolm. Wasn't aware this was one of your charities."

"This one only got off the ground five or six months ago. Had a long wait for the incorporation paperwork, since it's a nonprofit charitable corporation."

"Why aren't you listed as one of the owners?"

Malcolm cocked his head, a puzzled look on his face. "I am—wait, it's under Kris and my names. D.B.A. of Kristofer

Nicholas, right?"

"Those are the names Andrea found." Mina looked at him. "We never got a chance to go over our findings with you."

"Which is a damned shame, because I could have cleared up the misunderstanding and set your minds at ease. Malcolm Nicholas and his cousin, Jonah Kristofer, are well-known philanthropists. They support multiple charities and scholarship programs around the country."

He felt the corners of his lips tugging upward at the look of consternation on Mina's face. The urge to cup her cheeks in his hands, feel the heat of the beautiful blush spreading across them was almost too much to fight.

"Ms. McDaniels…" Malcolm said, before she interrupted.

"Please, call me Willie."

Gator felt himself preening like a fool because, though she'd allowed Malcolm the luxury of using her first name, she'd kept his special name for her separate. Everybody else could call her Willie, but he was the only one allowed to use Mina. And he liked that just fine.

"Willie said there's a problem with a few of the donations made by check to Holly Jolly."

"Three that we're aware of," Gator confirmed.

"I have all the spreadsheets on my laptop. Velma usually handles the data entry from each donation, though Patti takes the occasional one, and writes the receipt, but Velma enters those into the computer when she's doing the daily totals. The spreadsheet is transmitted to the main server, and

I make the deposit the next morning. The money is locked in the hotel's safe after hours, so nobody has access to the cash."

"You keep a donor's list? Is everyone on it?"

"Anybody donating by check, yes. Cash donations are often made without the donor waiting for a receipt, so they are listed as miscellaneous."

Gator rubbed his chin, puzzling out the steps Malcolm mentioned. "Has anybody else reported a discrepancy?"

Malcolm pulled out his phone. "Gimme a second, and I'll check." He punched in a number and waited. "Jonah, have there been any complaints about donations with Holly Jolly Holiday Helpers?"

He listened, his cheeks growing ruddy, and his gaze heated. "Thanks, I'll handle it." He turned to Gator. "Nobody has complained about any discrepancies with the finances."

"But? From the look on your face, something's wrong."

"We've got missing toys. A lot. We're talking possibly hundreds. The shop at The Great Escape is the main hub, but we've also got a couple of stops set up at fast food places where toys can be dropped off. They are collected and delivered to the hotel's shop to be inventoried and wrapped."

Willie brushed her fingers across Gator's arm, drawing his attention. "I wondered about that the last time I was in Holly Jolly's. The day before, there were stacks and stacks of things. Yesterday, it seemed like the amount had dwindled significantly." Turning to Malcolm, she shrugged. "I thought maybe they'd been moved to a central location, getting them ready to distribute."

"That's why it was brought to Jonah's attention. The supervisor making the pickups said the number of toys coming from this shop has steadily decreased every day. Something fishy is going on, and I'm going to get to the bottom of it."

Malcolm headed toward the shop, his scowl deepening. Gator reached and grabbed him by the arm.

"Wait. Before you go off half-cocked, I've got an idea."

Willie looked at him with a secretive smile. "I think we're on the same page." She pointed toward the ceiling, and he grinned.

"Cameras," they said simultaneously.

Breaking into a brisk walk, they headed toward the security office, ready to examine some after-hours footage and capture a crook.

Chapter Fifteen

The hotel lobby seemed eerily quiet after the congested festivities of Santa's Village. After hours, the lights were lowered, and the shops stood in silence, like ghostly echoes of the day's frenetic holiday pace.

Gator and Mina sat in front of a large panel of monitors, displaying closed circuit security camera feeds for The Great Escape. Earlier in the day they'd poured over hour after hour of footage for the cameras near Holly Jolly's. It was painstaking, like trying to find a needle in a haystack, to pinpoint anything outside the routine delivery of toys and presents for the charity. Lots of people going inside with goodies, and coming out empty-handed. Which was precisely what you'd expect. It wasn't until they'd rolled the afterhours footage that they'd hit the jackpot.

Every evening at precisely ten thirty-five p.m., a janitor's cart would stop in front of the shop. The woman pushing the cart glanced around before knocking softly on the window. Moments later the door opened—from the inside—and a large empty garbage can was rolled inside. Minutes later, the cleaning woman came out with the can loaded with a garbage bag—one that hadn't been in the can before she'd gone inside. The bag was tied closed, so it was impossible to tell what it held, but the cart and the trash can were immediately wheeled away from the shop and toward the employee's only area of the hotel.

Lucky for them, the hotel had CCTV cameras indoors and *outdoors*, so they had a bird's eye view of what occurred next. The sequence was crystal clear. Five minutes after the trash can left Holly Jolly's front door, Velma left the darkened store, locking the door behind her and leaving the hotel through the front.

Less than five minutes later, a car pulled up to the back of the hotel, where the trash collection and dumpsters were located, and the mystery bag passed from the trash can to the trunk of her car.

Tonight, between Gator, Mina, and Malcolm, they planned to catch her red-handed.

"It's almost ten thirty. Do you think she's going to show?" Mina's words were whispered, as she leaned closer to the monitor.

"You don't have to whisper, nobody's going to hear you except me." Gator stood and stretched. It felt like he'd been sitting for hours, and he was ready to get things cleared up. If his suspicions were right, they had two entirely different scenarios going on and by tomorrow morning, if they played their cards right, everything would be wrapped up in a nice little package, and he might finally be able to shed that Santa suit for good.

Mina grinned. "Sorry. I haven't been on a stakeout in…a very long time."

Hmm. There was another little piece of the puzzle that

was Wilhelmina McDaniels. Ordinary citizens didn't normally take part in stakeouts. He found her more and more fascinating every day.

"It shouldn't be long now, if they stick to their routine. Ah, look." He motioned to the camera. "Here comes our first player."

The cleaning lady pushed the laden cart over beside the front door, dragging the rolling trash can behind her. The hotel had decent cameras, so they were able to see the can was most definitely empty. It was also clear to see her hands were trembling.

The door to Holly Jolly eased open at the woman's knock and she pushed the trash can through, following it inside and closing the door. Too bad the interior of the store didn't have any cameras, but that row of storefronts normally wasn't shops at all, but office and conference room space that had been leased out to merchants for the holiday.

"There she is," Mina said, pointing to the camera. Sure enough, the cleaning woman came out, pulling the now full can behind here, and tugged the door closed.

"If she follows her pattern, she'll head toward the loading dock in the back, to *dump* the trash."

"And meet up with—ah, there she is. Our co-conspirator, Velma."

Gator pulled out his phone. "Malcolm, you in position?"

"Yes, and let me tell you, it's damned uncomfortable."

"Suck it up, buttercup. Velma's on her way. Mina and I are heading in for phase two."

Leaving the security office, they sprinted toward the back

of the hotel, where the rendezvous drop-offs took place. They could hear the squeaking wheels of the can being rolled down the ramp.

Headlights appeared around the corner of the hotel, and a dark blue sedan pulled up beside the dumpster. It was the same car they'd seen in the security footage. A quick check of the license plate earlier confirmed it belonged to Velma Whitehall.

The brakes squealed as the car stopped, and Velma jumped from behind the wheel. "We've gotta hurry. Something doesn't feel right."

"Look, this is the last time. I didn't want to do this in the first place."

Gator glanced over his shoulder at Mina, making sure they were both out of sight, but definitely not out of earshot. Sounded like the cleaning lady had a case of cold feet. Too little, too late at this point. She was in this up to her neck, same as Velma.

"Shut up! You took the money and you'll get the rest as soon as the toys sell. Quit your bellyaching, and grab that bag."

Velma pressed the key fob, and the trunk popped open—and Malcolm sat up, his usual dour scowl riding his face. Velma's shriek could be heard all the way to where Gator stood. His shoulders shook with laughter, and Mina elbowed him in the ribs.

"Hush," she whispered. "Let's go get the bad guys—I mean girls."

Malcolm climbed out of the trunk, and his hand latched

onto Velma's arm as she tried to run.

"Oh, no you don't. You've got some explaining to do."

"Please, mister. Here, take them. I'll be happy never to see them again." The cleaning lady yanked the plastic trash bag from the can, tugging so hard it caught and tore, spilling half the contents on the ground. A variety of expensive toys from the shop spilled onto the ground in a pile.

Gator pulled out his phone and hit a number on speed dial. "We've got 'em, you can come clean up the mess."

Within seconds, red and blue flashing lights spilled into the parking lot, though the sirens were silent. Officers took both women into custody, handcuffing them and placing them into separate police cars. The toys were collected and also placed in the cars to be held as evidence.

"I'm going to head downtown with my lawyers. We'll get the information from Velma to get back all the toys that haven't already been sold, and have everything taken off the sale sites." Malcolm dusted off his hands, reaching forward and clasping Mina's hand in his.

"Willie, I have to thank you for coming to me with your concerns." He grinned and his whole face lit up, and Gator couldn't help noticing the matching smile on Mina's face.

"Even if I suspected you of being the thief?" She chuckled before adding, "I'm glad I was wrong. You're doing a good thing, helping the less fortunate children."

"I agree," Gator added, pulling Mina against his side. He heard her quickly muffled gasp, but the message he sent Malcolm was loud and clear, and the other man nodded his acknowledgement. He wouldn't poach.

"I've got somebody looking into the discrepancy with the checks. I can't see Velma masterminding check fraud. I'll keep you posted, Malcolm."

"Thanks."

Without another word, he spoke with one of the police officers, before heading around to the front of the hotel, where his Mercedes was parked.

"Come on, Mina. I'll give you a ride home."

As they walked toward Gator's truck, she looked up at the sky. "It's a beautiful night, isn't it? Christmas is almost here. There's a chill in the air. Reminds me a bit of home."

"London?"

"A bit north, though I lived in London for a few years."

Another piece of the puzzle. He contemplated using one of his connections with The Agency—they still owed him a few favors—to check into her background, deeper than the superficial search he'd done in the beginning, when she'd first moved to New Orleans. But he wouldn't, because he wanted to unwrap the layers of Wilhelmina McDaniels himself, and discover the delights that lay beneath the surface.

"Yes, indeed, it's a beautiful night."

Chapter Sixteen

She opened blurry eyes, and stared at the bedside clock. Good heavens, it was barely six thirty in the morning. Who in the world pounded on her door at this hour? Especially since it was Christmas morning.

Shrugging into her robe, she pushed the hair out of her eyes and padded to the front door, ready to read the riot act to whoever was on the other side.

Gator stood there, holding up two cups of coffee and a brown paper bag filled with who knew what. He grinned at her scowl.

"What in the world are you doing here before the sun's even up?" She started to place her hands on her hips, then had to grab at the front of the robe as it started to slide open. *Oh, no! I am so not showing Gator my jiggly middle.*

Cinching the belt tighter, she groaned inwardly when she realized it was her ratty flannel robe, one she'd owned for years. It was too big now, but it was comfortable, and warm, and nobody—especially Gator Boudreau—was supposed to see her wearing it. And she ws pretty sure that she had a bad case of bed head. Her had quickly rose and patted at the tousled waves.

"I come bearing gifts. May I come in?"

She shrugged before opening the door wide enough for him to enter. "Fine, but I warn you, I'm not at my best this early in the morning."

"I'll try and remember that." The tiniest hint of a smile curved his lips, and his eyes sparkled with mirth.

Great, he's a morning person.

Chuckling, he handed her one of the cups and strolled across the hardwoods toward the kitchen counter, where he placed the brown paper bag, unfurling the folded over top. He pulled out something warm and golden brown, and the smell had her mouth watering. Her stomach rumbled loud enough she was afraid he heard it across the room.

"Since you're always feeding me," he gave her a wink, "I figured it was my turn to return the favor."

Still half-asleep, she ambled over to the bag and peered inside. "What is that?"

He leaned over the peninsula and grabbed a napkin, and placed the delicious-smelling concoction on top. "Taste it."

Eyeing it warily, she pulled off a corner and popped it into her mouth, moaning as the sweetness of maple syrup hit her tongue. She moaned, and pulled off another piece, chewing with her eyes closed.

"This is really good."

"I know a guy who owns a bakery. His stuff's not as good as yours, but..."

She opened her eyes, smiling demurely at the compliment. "I'm glad you like my baking, Gator."

Patting the bar stool beside him, he added, "Sit. I've got some news."

Settling onto the seat, she took a sip of the coffee, nearly choking on the powerful chicory flavor. "You may have good taste in baked goods, but your taste in coffee is abysmal."

He shrugged, though she saw the smile playing along his lips. "You'll get used to it."

"I doubt it," she muttered under her breath, putting the cup down. "You said you have news?"

"I had somebody at Abigail's bank looking into the mystery of her vanishing funds. Turns out it was a computer glitch at the bank, and there were about ten different accounts affected. For whatever reason, the balances were wiped out to zero. Abigail and her friends all bank at the same branch, and they just happened to be some of the unlucky ones. The glitch is fixed, and they all have the money back in their accounts. It was always there, but the computer showed the zero balances." He took a long drink of his coffee, and she watched his Adam's apple bob with each swallow. "If she'd gone in to the bank in person, it would have been handled the next day. Instead she panicked and called me—and you know the rest of the story."

"So it had nothing to do with Malcolm?"

"Other than being a gigantic coincidence? No."

Looking toward the window, she watched the sun rise, painting the sky with vivid oranges and reds and yellows. The wash of colors blended together like a watercolor painting by a master artist, and she realized again how much she'd grown to love her new home, and the city that was becoming a big part of her heart. With the dawn, came a renewed sense of well-being. It looked like today might be a glorious day.

"So everybody's Christmas is saved."

When Gator didn't say anything, she looked at him, and noted the mischievous twinkle in his eye, the one she was coming to recognize when he had something up his sleeve. The man was up to something, and she had a feeling she was about to be dragged smack dab into the middle of it.

And she didn't mind—not one little bit.

"I have another favor to ask…"

Epilogue

How had she gotten dragged into this? Oh, yeah, Gator showed up on her doorstep. Now, here she stood, dressed in her Mrs. Claus outfit one more time, even though the job officially ended the night before—Christmas Eve.

Gator tiptoed across the front porch of the single story ranch-style house in Metairie. It wasn't in the best shape, an older home probably built in the early sixties, and it had seen better days. Though it was evident the owners did the best they could. Even in the dead of winter, poinsettias in flower pots lined the front porch, their bright red and white blooms adding a joyful ambience and a little holiday cheer. The yard was raked free of fallen leaves, and the gate hadn't squeaked when they'd opened it.

"Go ahead and ring the doorbell, Mina."

She watched Gator lift two red bags higher onto his shoulder, and settle himself on the porch swing, placing the bags on the seat beside him.

Bless his heart. He's just a big old softie.

Straightening the blasted corset once again, she pressed the doorbell, and heard children's high-pitched voices calling out, and the scamper of little feet.

Within seconds, the front door was flung open, and

Frankie stood open-mouthed, surprise stamped on his cute freckled features. Hannah, racing up behind him, slammed into him, and landed with a thud on her backside.

"Hi, Mrs. Santa." Frankie gave a tentative glance past her shoulder, obviously looking for somebody, and she had a pretty good idea who.

"Merry Christmas, Frankie. Merry Christmas, Hannah." Willie smiled at their mother standing a few feet behind them, open-mouthed with surprise.

"Mrs. Santa!" Hannah pushed past her brother, throwing her tiny arms around Willie's waist and squeezing tight. She chuckled, patting the little one's back. Well, well. She certainly hadn't expected such an enthusiastic welcome.

"Mr. Claus and I were on our way back to the North Pole, and realized we had something we forgot to deliver last night. Do you think you could help us?"

"Sure."—"I wanna help." Frankie and Hannah grabbed her hands, and she backed up a step, tugging them onto the porch.

"Good morning, Frankie, Hannah. Merry Christmas." Gator's voice carried across the porch, infused with warmth and cheer.

"Santa!" Pulling free from Willie's hand, Hannah raced across the porch, her little bare feet barely making a sound. With a laugh, she flung herself against Gator, hard enough the swing rocked back several inches. Frankie stayed by Willie's side, eyes wary. Poor little tyke.

Leaning forward, Willie whispered in his ear. "Frankie, go ahead. Everything's going to be okay."

As if her words freed the tether around his fear, Frankie raced across the porch, wrapping his arms around Gator's neck and holding on tight. Gator's softly murmured words were muffled, but she could imagine precisely what he said. For a man with such a gruff exterior, Gator Boudreau really did have a heart of gold, and a soft spot for children.

"Hey, Santa! Your bag is moving!"

"Well, now, so it is. I wonder what's inside." Gator opened the drawstring top of the first bag and peered inside. "My goodness, how'd you get in there?" He lifted the squirming bag and handed it to Hannah. "I think this is for you, sweetie."

"Me?" Hannah looked into the open bag and squealed, the shrieking sound causing her mother to rush further across the porch.

"Hannah?" Her gaze flitted between Willie and Gator, filled with questions. Willie wrapped an arm around her shoulder and whispered in her ear, patting her shoulder when tears began falling down her cheeks.

Through it all, Frankie stood silent, watching as Hannah pulled a little orange and white striped tabby kitten from Santa's bag, rubbing her face against its soft fur.

"Thank you, Santa!"

"Frankie, this one's for you." Gator handed him the other bag, which wiggled and moved and a little barking yip sounded from inside.

"It's for...me?"

"I told you, what happened wasn't your fault, son. But I want your promise you'll be extra careful and watch over both your pets and your baby sister, okay?"

"Yes, sir." Frankie pulled a squirming black bundle from the sack, all big paws and a lolling pink tongue, which immediately began licking his face. The laughter spilling from his lips made this Christmas morning special, and Mina blinked back tears, knowing she wasn't hiding her emotions from Gator's sideways look.

"Well, we've got to get back to the North Pole. No telling what kind of mischief those elves have been up to while we've been gone." Reaching down, Gator ruffled Frankie's hair, before patting Hannah atop her head. "Merry Christmas."

Willie couldn't hear what he whispered to their mother, but she nodded and mouthed *thank you* before kneeling down beside Hannah, still running her fingers across the kitten's soft fur.

"Let's go," he said softly, taking Willie's hand and helping her down the three steps leading to the walkway.

"You are a very nice man, Gator Boudreau."

"Don't go spreading it around, Mina. It'll ruin my reputation."

She stopped while he opened the front gate, and waited until he met her gaze. Not knowing if she'd ever get the chance again, she leaned forward and pressed a kiss against his lips.

"Merry Christmas, Gator."

He lifted his hands and cupped her cheeks between them, staring deeply into her eyes. She didn't look away, letting him read everything she felt at that moment.

"Merry Christmas, Mina McDaniels. May this be the first of many."

His lips crashed down on hers, and he pulled her closer, his body pressed against hers, the fake whiskers tickling against her cheeks. Yet this kiss held both a promise and a depth of passion she hadn't felt in a very long time.

"Look, Momma, Santa is kissing Mrs. Claus!"

"I see that, Hannah. Let's all go inside and have Christmas breakfast. I think Santa and Mrs. Claus need to get home—or find a room away from prying little eyes."

Willie's whole body shook with laughter at the mother's parting words, but she'd heard the humor and good-natured ribbing underlying them. Resting her forehead against Gator's chest, he pulled her tighter against him, wrapping his arms around her and holding her close.

"I meant to ask, how'd you get the puppy and kitten so quickly? It is Christmas day."

Gator chuckled, "I know this guy. Red suit, white beard, big belly. Maybe you know him? He owed me a favor."

Chuckling, Willie leaned back in his arms, smiling. "Merry Christmas, Santa."

Dear Reader:

Are you ready for even more New Orleans Connection Series? Fatal Intentions is coming soon! This is Jean-Luc Boudreau's story, and here's a little excerpt to tide you over until release day. And at the end of the excerpt, there's a pre-order button, if you want to grab it now and have it delivered to your ereader the day it releases.

FATAL INTENTIONS © Kathy Ivan (New Orleans Connection Series #6)

Less than two feet away, the gorgeous blonde glowered at Jean-Luc like he was the pile of steaming dog poo she'd just plopped her four-inch heel into. Hey, not his problem. He'd been minding his own business, sitting on his father's back porch, enjoying a cold beer when she'd climbed out of her car, demanding he come with her. *Right.* She might be cute as a caterpillar, but it wasn't happening. He was eyeballs deep in the ongoing EryX Pharmaceutical debacle Carpenter Security Services was currently working on, and this was the first time he'd stopped long enough to take a deep breath.

His entire perspective did a one-eighty the moment she uttered two little words. Words which not only changed his mind, but had him halfway to her car before he realized he'd taken the first step.

"What did you say?" His voice held a forceful demand, and he didn't give a damn whether she liked his tone or not. She'd been the one who'd showed up unannounced, spewing demands.

Her brown eyes flashed with an inner fire, while her navy blue and white-shod toes tapped on the brittle grass. This late in December, it was mostly brown anyway, hibernating for the coming spring.

"Which part of the sentence are you having difficulty with, Mr. Boudreau? Was it the part where I politely asked you to get in the car and come with me?"

"Chére, you haven't uttered a polite word since you opened the car door and stepped onto my drive. Which, I might add, is private property." He almost chuckled as she tossed a swathe of blonde curls over her shoulder, with a brown-eyed glare. He couldn't help thinking about the old saying, *if looks could kill…*

"You are such an ass," she muttered sotto voce, though still loud enough he heard her quite clearly. Inhaling a deep breath, she gave him a polite smile—one that came nowhere close to reaching those whiskey-colored eyes and pasted on a smile.

"I'm sorry if I've been rude, Mr. Boudreau. Can we start again?"

"Forget rude. I want to know what you meant telling me my wife is dying."

PREORDER LINK:

www.tinyurl.com/kivanbooks

NEWSLETTER SIGN UP

Don't want to miss out on any new books, contests, and free stuff? Sign up to get my newsletter. I promise not to spam you, and only send out notifications/e-mails whenever there's a new release or contest/giveaway.

http://eepurl.com/baqdRX

REVIEWS ARE IMPORTANT!

People are always asking how they can help spread the word about my books. One of the best ways to do that is by word of mouth. Telling your friends about the books and recommending them. If you find a book or series or author that you love – talk about it. The next best thing is to write a review. Writing a review for a book doesn't have to be long or detailed. It can be as simple as saying "I loved the book."

I hope you enjoyed reading Spies Like Us. If you liked the story, I hope you'll consider leaving a review for the book at the vendor where you purchased it and at Goodreads. Reviews are the best way to spread the word to others looking for good books. It truly helps.

Deadly Justice © Kathy Ivan
(New Orleans Connection Series)

A quest for justice...

After a devastating betrayal, ex-DEA agent Samuel "*The Ghost*" Carpenter devotes his life to searching for the person who cost him not only his job but nearly his life. When he discovers a link between the man he's hunting and a beautiful executive assistant, he realizes the path to his target is seduction—a task he's all too eager to undertake, since he can't seem to resist the alluring beauty.

...turns into a dangerous seduction.

Andrea Kirkland can't fathom the sudden interest rich and powerful Samuel Carpenter's showing, but she's not stupid. He's got a deeply-hidden agenda and she's a means to an end. Except, she has secrets of her own, and despite their instantaneous chemistry, she's not above using Carpenter to further her own vendetta.

On a whirlwind journey from Dallas to New Orleans, passion explodes between them. But when a murderer strikes, Carpenter must choose between his mission of vengeance or face losing the woman he loves to a vindictive madman hellbent on revenge.

Get it Now!

BOOKS BY KATHY IVAN

www.kathyivan.com/books.html

NEW ORLEANS CONNECTION SERIES
Desperate Choices
Connor's Gamble
Relentless Pursuit
Ultimate Betrayal
Keeping Secrets
Sex, Lies and Apple Pies
Deadly Justice
Saving Sarah (part of Susan Stoker's Special Forces Kindle World)
Deadly Obsession
Hidden Agenda
Saving Savannah (part of Susan Stoker's Special Forces Kindle World)
Spies Like Us
Fatal Intentions (coming February 2017)

LOVIN' LAS VEGAS SERIES
It Happened In Vegas
Crazy Vegas Love
Marriage, Vegas Style
A Virgin In Vegas
Vegas, Baby!
Yours For The Holidays
Match Made In Vegas
Wicked Wagers (box set books 1-4)

OTHER BOOKS BY KATHY IVAN
Second Chances (Destiny's Desire Book #1)
Losing Cassie (Destiny's Desire Book #2)
The Remingtons: Could This Be Love (Part of Melissa
Foster's Kindle World)

MEET KATHY IVAN

USA TODAY Bestselling author Kathy Ivan spent most of her life with her nose between the pages of a book. It didn't matter if the book was a paranormal romance, romantic suspense, action and adventure thrillers, sweet & spicy, or a sexy novella. Kathy turned her obsession with reading into the next logical step, writing. Her books transport you to the sultry splendor of the French Quarter in New Orleans in her award-winning romantic suspense, or to Las Vegas in her contemporary romantic comedies. Kathy tells stories people can't get enough of; reuniting old loves, betrayal of trust, finding kidnapped children, psychics and even a ghost or two. But one thing they all have in common – love (and some pretty steamy sex scenes too). You can find more on Kathy at

WEBSITE:
www.kathyivan.com

FACEBOOK:
facebook.com/kathyivanauthor

TWITTER:
twitter.com/@kathyivan

EDITORIAL REVIEWS AND AUTHOR QUOTES

"Kathy Ivan's books are addictive, you can't read just one!"

—Susan Stoker,
NYT and USA TODAY Bestselling Author

"Kathy Ivan's books give you everything you're looking for and so much more".

—Geri Foster,
USA Today and NYT Bestselling Author of
the Falcon Securities Series

"This is the first I have read from Kathy Ivan and it won't be the last."

—Night Owl Reviews

"I highly recommend Desperate Choices. Readers can't go wrong here!"

—Melissa, Joyfully Reviewed

"I loved how the author wove a very intricate storyline with plenty of intriguing details that led to the final reveal…"

—Night Owl Reviews

Desperate Choices—Winner 2012 International Digital Award—Suspense

Desperate Choices—Best of Romance 2011 –Joyfully Reviewed

Printed in Great Britain
by Amazon